Stories of D and Mystery

Selected and simplified by
E. J. H. Morris and D. J. Mortimer

Introduction and questions by
Rowena Akinyemi

Longman

Acknowledgements

We are indebted to the following for permission to reproduce simplified versions of copyright material:

The author and her agents Curtis Brown Ltd for "Family Affair" by Margery Allingham; Edward Arnold (Publishers) Ltd for "The Mezzotint" from *Collected Ghost Stories* by M. R. James; the author and her agents Hughes Massie Limited for "Philomel Cottage" by Agatha Christie; Mrs A. A. Gordon Clark and Messrs Faber & Faber Ltd for "The Heel" by Cyril Hare from *Best Detective Stories of Cyril Hare*; Miss D. E. Collins and Messrs Cassell & Co. Ltd for "The Blue Cross" and "The Invisible Man" from *The Innocence of Father Brown* by G. K. Chesterton; W. Foulsham & Co. Ltd for "The Unlucky Theatre", originally entitled "The Hoodoo Theatre" by Elliott O'Donnell; Messrs Hutchinson & Co. (Publishers) Ltd for "The Case of the Thing that Whimpered" from *Gunmen, Gallants and Ghosts* by Dennis Wheatley, and the author and Victor Gollancz Ltd for "The Great Idea of Mr Budd", originally entitled "The Inspiration of Mr Budd" from *In the Teeth of the Evidence* by Dorothy L. Sayers.

Contents

Introduction

"The detective story was . . . very much a story with a moral; in fact it was . . . the hunting down of Evil and the triumph of Good." The stories in this collection illustrate in a variety of ways these words of Agatha Christie (*An Autobiography*, 1977). The detective and mystery short story does not concern itself with complex themes. The aspect of human experience which the stories in this collection investigate is the fact that things are not always as they seem. Ordinary observation is not always reliable; the unexpected can in reality be commonplace; or, on the other hand, the ordinary can hide the horrific. These stories are all examples of the classic detective and mystery story: they all end with the defeat of evil, or the explanation of mystery, and the restoration of order.

Agatha Christie (1890–1976) published her first novel in 1920 and went on to publish seventy-seven books in her lifetime. Several of these were romantic novels, and she wrote some short stories and several successful plays, but detective stories were by far her most popular books.

Although "Philomel Cottage" is unlike Agatha Christie's usual mystery story — there is no detective, no group of suspects, no clues — it illustrates clearly her sympathy with the victim of crime. "I have got more interest in my victims than my criminals," she wrote in her autobiography. "The more passionately alive the victim, the more glorious indignation I have on his behalf, and am full of a delighted triumph when I have delivered a near-victim out of the shadow of death."

In "Philomel Cottage", Alix Martin is delivered out of the shadow of death. The story is told from her point of view, as her suspicions against her husband are gradually aroused. The seeds of suspicion are sown in the first few paragraphs of the story: "'The man's a complete stranger to you! You know nothing about him!'" Gradually, Alix's belief in Gerald's sincerity is eroded by sinister discoveries. The suspense in the early part of the story is created by the mystery of who Gerald is; later it is provided by Alix's dangerous situation and finally Alix watches the evil Gerald "ready to spring upon her".

The novels of Dorothy L. Sayers (1893–1957) are best known for her popular amateur detective Lord Peter Wimsey, but in the story "The Great Idea of Mr Budd" it is an ordinary barber, Mr Budd, who defeats the murderer William Strickland. There is no gradual revelation of the evil which Strickland personifies; the suspense of the story is created first of all by the doubt about the identity of the stranger in the barber's shop, and then by Mr Budd's attempt to outwit the murderer. It is Mr Budd's success which ends the story: "'The *great* Mr Budd? I think that you're *quite* wonderful . . .'"

The detective story was confined in its early days to the form of the short story. G. K. Chesterton (1874–1936) wrote his detective fiction solely in the short story form. Chesterton was one of the best-known journalists in the United Kingdom and was the author of books of literary criticism, poetry and theology before he turned to the detective story. He published forty-eight short stories about Father Brown between 1911 and 1935. Father Brown is unique in detective fiction, and yet some of his characteristics were used by other authors in the creation of their own amateur detectives.

Father Brown's name, the first indication of the ordinary, inconspicuous nature of Chesterton's detective, contrasts with the exotic names of other characters in the stories (Flambeau, Valentin, Isidore Smythe). "The little priest had a round, dull face; he had eyes as empty as the North Sea; he had several parcels wrapped in brown paper, which he was quite unable to collect together." But Father Brown reveals himself as not quite the simple priest he seems, as he misleads the famous French criminal in "The Blue Cross", and solves the mystery of "The Invisible Man". His knowledge of human nature and his flair for unusual methods of detection are illustrated in "The Blue Cross";

and his very simplicity enables him to see what others miss in "The Invisible Man", as he exposes the supernatural mystery as a careless error of thought.

Albert Campion, the amateur detective created by Margery Allingham (1904–1966), appears in many of her novels as well as in the short story "Family Affair". The details of Campion's character, like those of Father Brown, are left vague. He, too, gives the impression of being foolish. "Campion, who was quiet and fair and wore glasses, listened attentively as his habit was. And, as usual, he looked hesitant and a little uncertain of himself; a great many men had failed to regard him seriously until it was too late." Campion solves the mystery of the empty house by revealing, like Father Brown in "The Invisible Man", a commonsense solution.

In the traditional detective story, the police are part of the plot, but they are always subordinate to the detective in the solution of the mystery. In "The Great Idea of Mr Budd", the police take an active part in the arrest of murderer William Strickland, but that is their only function in the story: "The policemen rushed forward. There was a shout and a shot, which went harmlessly through the window, and the passenger was brought out." Similarly, in "Philomel Cottage" it is Dick Windyford who comes to rescue Alix and the police play a secondary role: "Then he turned to the man with him, a tall strong policeman. 'Go and see what's happening in that room.'"

In "The Blue Cross", the head of the Paris police, Valentin, plodding across London behind Father Brown, offers a striking contrast to the priest. He does not understand what is happening until Father Brown explains. Valentin then turns to the criminal Flambeau: "'Do not bow to me, my friend . . . let us bow to our master.' And they both stood for a moment with their hats off, while the little Essex priest searched about for his umbrella."

The police do not play a part in "The Invisible Man", but Flambeau (now reformed, and working as a private detective) serves as a contrast to Father Brown. Flambeau's room is "ornamented with swords and weapons of all kinds, strange objects from the East, bottles of Italian wine . . . ". Father Brown is "a small, dusty-looking priest who did not look quite right in these surroundings". Flambeau is aggressive in action: he runs upstairs to Smythe's flat and "clearly wanted to break the door with his big shoulder". Father Brown, on the other hand, "still stood and looked about him in the snow-covered street, as if he had lost interest in his inquiry". And yet, of course, it is Father Brown who solves the mystery, while Flambeau remains perplexed: "'Oh, this will drive me mad . . . Who is this fellow? What does he look like? What is the usual dress of a man who is invisible to the mind?'"

The policeman in "Family Affair", Chief Inspector Charles Luke, plays a prominent part in many of Margery Allingham's novels. He contrasts strikingly with Campion: "a dark, tough and very active man; and as usual he was talking continuously, using his hands to add force to his words." It is Campion, however, who solves the mystery in "Family Affair"; Luke, like Flambeau, has to ask the amateur for an explanation: "'I was completely fooled by it . . . You know, Campion, you were right . . . How did you guess the solution?'"

In "The Heel", by Cyril Hare (1900–1958), it is the policeman who plays the role of the detective in the story: Sergeant Place notices the tiny clue and solves the mystery. None of the characters in this story are described in any depth. The most we learn about Place is that his "smile usually made people feel at ease". The discovery of the murderer leads Place to remark cheerfully that he will soon be dead. The victim is described as "the poor harmless servant". The classic detective story, relying on the solution of a puzzle as the whole purpose of its plot, dispenses with detailed characterisation, as "The Heel" perfectly illustrates.

In later detective and mystery fiction, the character of the murderer or criminal became a more important part of the story, but at the time these stories were written most writers shared the view of Agatha Christie: "I was, like everyone else who wrote books or read them, *against* the criminal and *for* the innocent victim." Chesterton was the only exception. Father Brown is interested not so much in the defeat of evil and the arrest of the criminal as in the way men's minds work. In "The Invisible Man", Flambeau, the "great" criminal, has become a private detective. And at the end of the story, Father Brown, instead of bringing in the police to make an arrest, "walked those snow-covered hills under the stars for many hours with a murderer. What they said to each other will never be known."

Dennis Wheatley (1897–1977) was a prolific writer of novels on the supernatural, and in "The Case of the Thing that Whimpered", his interest in the supernatural is personified by Neils Orsen, who "had chosen to spend his life in the study of ghosts and spirits". The supernatural events which occur in Mark Hemmingway's new storehouse are so violent that Orsen says: "'I really believe now that we're on the track of an *Ab-human* . . . a bodiless force — something that has somehow made its way up out of the Great Depths and found a gateway by which it can get back into this world.'" However, the unexpected ending restores order and provides a commonsense solution to the mystery, in the classic tradition of detective mysteries.

"The Mezzotint" and "The Unlucky Theatre" are the only two stories in this collection which offer a supernatural solution to their mysteries. In "The Mezzotint", a crime of a previous generation is solved by the observation of the changes in the picture. Order is restored once the crime has been revealed: ". . . it was an uncommon picture. And although it was watched with great care, it has never been known to change again." In "The Unlucky Theatre", order is restored only when the theatre is pulled down.

It is the restoration of order, following the defeat of evil, the solution of a puzzle or the explanation of a mystery, which gives detective stories their form. As Margery Allingham wrote, the popularity of the mystery story is "a sign of the popular instinct for order and form".

The Blue Cross
by G. K. Chesterton

Early one morning the boat arrived at Harwich and let loose a crowd of travellers like flies, among whom the man that we must follow was in no way unusual. Nor did he wish to be. There was nothing extraordinary about him, except a slight difference between the holiday gaiety of his clothes and the official, solemn expression of his face. His clothes included a pale grey coat, a white waistcoat, and a silver hat made of straw with a grey-blue ribbon round it. Compared with his clothes his thin face was dark and ended in a short black beard. He was smoking. No one would have thought that the grey coat covered a loaded gun, that the white waistcoat covered a police card, or that the hat covered one of the most powerful brains in Europe. For this was Valentin himself, the head of the Paris police and the most famous detective in the world; and he was coming from Brussels to London to make the greatest arrest of the century.

Flambeau was in England. The police of three countries had tracked the great criminal at last from Ghent to Brussels, from Brussels to the Hook of Holland; and it was thought that he would make some criminal use of the strangeness and confusion of the meeting of priests from all over the world, which was then being held in London. Probably he would travel as some unimportant clerk or secretary connected with it; but, of course, Valentin could not be certain; nobody could be certain about Flambeau.

It is many years now since this great criminal, Flambeau, suddenly stopped bringing trouble and disturbance into the world; and when he stopped there was great quiet upon the earth. But in his best days (I mean, of course, his worst) Flambeau was an internationally well-known figure. Almost every morning people read in their daily papers that he had escaped punishment for one extraordinary crime by breaking the law a second time. He was a Frenchman of great strength and size who often showed great daring; and the wildest stories were told of the amusing uses that he made of his strength; how he turned a judge upside down and stood him on his head, "to clear his mind"; how he ran down the street with a policeman under each arm. It must be said of him, however, that his extraordinary bodily strength was generally employed in bloodless though hardly noble scenes. Each of his robberies would make a story by itself. It was he who ran the great Tyrolean Milk Company in London, with no cows, no carts, and no milk, but with more than a thousand people who bought from him. He did this by the simple operation of moving the little milk-cans outside people's doors to the doors of the people he was supposed to serve. A great simplicity, however, could be seen in many of his crimes. It is said that he once repainted all the numbers on the doors of the houses in a street in the middle of the night merely to lead one traveller into a trap. It is quite certain that he invented a public letterbox, which he was able to move. This he put up at quiet corners of the town because there was a chance that a stranger might drop a letter containing money into it. Lastly, he was known to be very active and quick; although his body was so large, he could jump as well as any insect and hide in the treetops like a monkey. For this reason the great Valentin, when he set out to find Flambeau, knew very well that his adventures would not end when he found him.

But how was he to find him? On this the great Valentin's ideas were still not settled.

There was one thing which Flambeau could not cover, even though he was very skilful at dressing to look like someone else, and that was his unusual height. If Valentin's quick eye had seen a tall apple-seller, a tall soldier, or even a fairly tall woman, he might have arrested them immediately. But just as an elephant cannot pretend to be a cat, so there was nobody on his train who could be Flambeau dressed as someone else. Valentin had already made certain that he was not among the people on the boat; and only six other people had got on the train at Harwich or on the journey. There was a short railway official travelling up to London, three fairly short farmers picked up two stations afterwards, one very short widow lady going up from a town in Essex, and a very short priest going up from an Essex village. When it came to the last case, Valentin gave up looking and almost laughed. The little priest had a round, dull face; he had eyes as empty as the North Sea; he had several parcels wrapped in brown paper, which he was quite unable to collect together. The meeting of priests in London must have brought out of their quiet villages many such creatures who seemed blind and helpless like underground animals which have been dug out of the earth. This one would have made anyone feel pity for him. He had a large, worn umbrella, which kept falling on the floor. He explained with foolish simplicity to everybody in the carriage that he had to be careful, because he had something made of real silver "with blue stones" in one of his brown-paper parcels. His mixture of Essex dullness and priest's simplicity continuously amused the Frenchman until this simple man arrived (somehow) at Stratford with all his parcels, and came back for his umbrella. When he did this last thing, Valentin even had the good nature to warn him not to take care of his silver by telling everybody about it. But to whomever he talked, Valentin watched for someone else: he looked out steadily for anyone, rich or poor, male or female, who was at least six feet tall; for Flambeau was six inches above this height.

He got off the train in London, however, quite sure that he had not missed the criminal so far. When he had been to Scotland Yard to arrange for help if it was needed, he went for a long walk in the streets of London. As he went through the streets and squares beyond the area known as Victoria, he stopped suddenly. It was a quiet, rather unusual square, of the kind often found in London. The tall, flat houses in it looked both wealthy and empty; the square of bushes in the centre looked as lonely as a little Pacific island. One of the four sides of the square was much higher than the rest, like a stage; and the line of this side was broken by a restaurant. It stood specially high above the street, and some steps ran up from the street to the front door. Valentin stood in front of the yellow-white curtains and studied them for a long time.

Aristide Valentin was a thinking man and a plain man at the same time. All his wonderful successes, that looked like wonders, had been gained by slow, patient reasoning, by clear and ordinary French thought. But exactly because Valentin understood reason, he understood the limits of reason. Only a man who knows nothing about motors talks of driving without oil; only a man who knows nothing of reason talks of reasoning without any facts to start with. Flambeau had been missed at Harwich; and if he was in London at all, he might be anything — a tall beggar sleeping in one of the parks, or a tall official at the Metropole Hotel. When he lacked such certain knowledge, Valentin had a view and a system of his own.

In such cases he trusted in the unexpected. In such cases, when he could not follow a reasonable course, he coldly and carefully followed an unreasonable one. Instead of going to the right places, banks, police stations, meeting places — he went to the wrong places; he knocked at every empty house, turned down every little street leading nowhere, went up every little-used path blocked with rubbish. He defended this strange course quite reasonably. He said that if he had any facts about the criminal's movements to guide him, this was the worst way; but if he had no facts at all it was the best, because there was just the chance that anything unusual which caught the eye of the hunter might be the same that had caught the eye of the man he was hunting. Somewhere a man must begin, and it had better be just where another man might stop. Something about the steps leading up to the shop, something about the quiet and rather unusual appearance of the restaurant, made a strange idea grow in the detective's mind and made him decide to act without a plan. He went up the steps, sat down and asked for a cup of coffee. Until his coffee came, he sat in deep thought about Flambeau. The criminal always had the advantage; he could make his plans and act, while the detective could only wait and hope that he would make a mistake.

Valentin lifted his coffee cup to his lips slowly and put it down very quickly. He had put salt in it. He looked at the container from which the white powder had come. It was certainly a sugar basin. He wondered why they should put salt in it. He looked to see if there were any more of the kind of containers usually found on a table in a restaurant. Yes, there were two salt containers quite full. Perhaps there was something unusual about what was in them, too. He tasted it. It was sugar. Then he looked round at the restaurant with fresh interest, to see if there were any other signs of that strange artistic taste which puts sugar in the salt containers and salt in the sugar basins. Except for one or two stains of some dark liquid on one of the white walls, the whole place appeared neat, cheerful and ordinary. He rang the bell for the waiter.

When the waiter hurried up to him his hair looked rather untidy and his eyes rather tired at that early hour. The detective asked him to taste the sugar and see if it was equal to the high reputation of the restaurant. The result was that the waiter suddenly woke up.

"Do you play this fine joke on people every morning?" inquired Valentin. "Do you never grow tired of the joke of changing the salt and the sugar?"

When it became clear to the waiter what Valentin meant, he explained that the restaurant certainly had no such intention. It must be a strange mistake. He picked up the sugar basin and looked at it. He picked up the salt container and looked at that, and his face grew more and more surprised and puzzled. At last he quickly excused himself, hurried away, and in a few seconds returned with the manager. The manager also examined the sugar basin and then the salt container. The manager also looked surprised and puzzled.

Suddenly the waiter started to speak with a rush of words.

"I think," he said eagerly, "I think it is those two priests."

"What two priests?"

"The two priests who threw soup at the wall," said the waiter.

"Threw soup at the wall?" repeated Valentin.

"Yes, yes," said the waiter with excitement and pointed at the dark stain on the white wall. "Threw it over there on the wall."

Valentin looked a question at the manager, who came to the rescue with fuller reports.

"Yes, sir," he said, "it's quite true, although I don't suppose it has anything to do with the sugar and salt. The two priests came in and drank soup here very early, as soon as the doors were opened. They were both very quiet. One of them paid the bill and went out. The other, who seemed much slower, was some minutes longer collecting his things together. But he went at last. Only, the instant before he stepped into the street, he picked up his cup, which he had only half emptied, and threw the soup straight on the wall. I was in the back room myself, and so was the waiter; so I could only rush out in time to find the wall stained, and the shop empty. It didn't do any particular damage, but it was a very rude and surprising thing for a priest to do. I tried to catch the men in the street. They were too far off though. I only noticed that they went round the corner into Carstairs Street."

The detective was on his feet, with his hat settled on his head and his stick in his hand. He paid his bill, closed the glass doors loudly behind him, and was soon walking round into the next street.

It was fortunate that even in such moments of excitement his eye was cool and quick. Something in the front of a shop went by him like a flash; yet he went back to look at it. The shop was one which sold fruit, and piles of fruit were arranged in the open air with tickets on them plainly showing their names and prices. Right in the front were two heaps, one of oranges and the other of nuts. On the heap of nuts lay a ticket on which was written clearly in blue chalk, "Best oranges, two a penny," On the oranges was the equally clear and exact description, "Finest nuts, four pence a pound". Valentin looked at these two tickets and thought that he had met this kind of joke before, and that he had done so rather recently. He drew the attention of the red-faced shopkeeper, who seemed in a bad temper and was looking up and down the street, to the mistake in his advertisements. The shopkeeper said nothing, but quickly put each card into its proper place. The detective leaned on his walking stick and continued to look closely at the shop. At last he said, "Please excuse me, but I should like to ask you a question."

The red-faced shopkeeper looked at him in an unfriendly way, but the detective continued to lean on his walking-stick. "If two tickets are wrongly placed in a fruit shop," he went on, "in what way are they like a priest's hat that has come to London for a holiday? Or, in case I do not make myself clear, why has the thought come into my head which connects the idea of nuts marked oranges with the idea of two priests, one tall and the other short?"

The eyes of the shopkeeper stood out. For an instant he really seemed likely to throw himself on the stranger. At last he said angrily, "I don't know what you have to do with it. But you can tell them from me that I'll knock their stupid heads off, even though they are priests, if they upset my apples again."

"Indeed?" asked the detective, with great sympathy. "Did they upset your apples?"

"One of them did," said the angry shopkeeper. "He rolled them all over the street. I would have caught the fool if I hadn't had to pick them up."

"Which way did these priests go?" asked Valentin.

"Up that second road on the left-hand side, and then across the square," said the other promptly.

"Thanks," said Valentin, and moved off quickly. On the other side of the second square he found a policeman, and said, "This is urgent. Have you seen two priests?"

The policeman began to laugh heavily. "I have, sir. And if you want my opinion, one of them had had too much to drink. He stood in the middle of the road so confused that——"

"Which way did they go?" asked Valentin quickly.

"They went on one of those yellow buses over there," answered the man. "Those that go to Hampstead."

Valentin produced his official card and said very rapidly, "Call two of your men to come with me to follow these people." In a minute and a half the French detective was joined on the opposite side of the road by an inspector and a policeman in ordinary clothes.

"Well, sir," began the inspector, "and what may——?"

Valentin pointed with his stick. "I'll tell you on the top of that bus," he said, and ran through the confusion of the busy street. When all three sat, breathing heavily, on the top seats of the yellow bus, the inspector said "We could go four times as quickly in a taxi."

"Quite true," replied the leader calmly, "if we only had an idea of where we were going."

"Well, where *are* you going?" asked the other.

Valentin smoked his cigarette for a few seconds with a worried expression on his face. Then he said, "If you *know* what a man is doing, get in front of him. But if you want to *guess* what he's doing, keep behind him. Wander when he wanders. Stop when he stops. Travel as slowly as he does. Then you may see what he saw, and you may act as he acted. All we can do is to look very carefully for an unusual thing."

"What sort of unusual thing do you mean?" asked the inspector.

"Any sort of unusual thing," answered Valentin, and became silent.

The yellow bus went slowly up the northern roads for what seemed like hours. The great detective would explain no further, and perhaps the other two felt a silent and growing doubt about his purpose. Perhaps, also, they felt a silent and growing desire for lunch, for the time crept long past the ordinary lunch hour. The long roads on the northern edge of London seemed to stretch on and on. But although the winter sun was already beginning to set, the French detective still sat silent and watchful, and looked out at the shops and houses of the streets that slid by on either side. By the time that they had left Camden Town behind, the policemen were nearly asleep. At least they gave something like a jump as Valentin got up suddenly, struck a hand on each man's shoulder, and shouted to the driver to stop.

They almost fell down the steps and onto the road, and hardly realised that they had left their seats. When they looked round for an explanation, they found Valentin pointing his finger in excitement towards a window on the left side of the road. It was a large window, which formed part of the long front of a hotel. It was the part reserved for dining, and marked "Restaurant". The window was broken, with a big, black hole in it, like a star in the ice.

"Our sign at last," cried Valentin, waving his stick. "The place with the broken window."

"What window? What sign?" asked the inspector. "Why, what proof is there that this has anything to do with them?"

Valentin almost broke his stick in anger.

"Proof!" he cried. "Good heavens! the man is looking for proof! Why, of course, it is most unlikely that it has anything to do with them. But what else can we do? Don't you see we must either follow one wild possibility or else go home to bed?" He entered the restaurant with a great deal of noise and his companions followed. They were soon eating a late lunch at a little table, and looking at the star of broken glass from inside. Even then they could learn little from it.

"You've had your window broken, I see," Valentin said to the waiter, as he paid the bill.

"Ah, yes, sir," the waiter answered. "A very strange thing that, sir."

"Indeed? Tell us about it," said the detective.

"Well, two gentlemen in black came in," said the waiter. "Two of those priests who are filling the city at the moment. They had a cheap and quiet little lunch, and one of them paid for it and went out. The other was just going out to join him when I looked at my change again and found that he had paid me more than three times too much. 'Here,' I said to the priest who was nearly out of the door, 'you've paid too much,' 'Oh,' he said, 'have we?' 'Yes,' I said, and I picked up the bill to show him. Well, that was a real surprise."

"What do you mean?" asked Valentin.

"Well, I was sure that I put four shillings on that bill. But now I saw quite clearly that it was fourteen shillings."

"Well?" cried Valentin.

"The priest at the door said quite calmly, 'Sorry to confuse your accounts, but it will pay for the window.' 'What window?' I said. 'The one that I am going to break.' he said, and broke the window with his umbrella."

The inspector said quietly, "Are we after escaped madmen?" The waiter went on with enjoyment of the extraordinary story:

"I was so surprised for a second that I couldn't do anything. The man marched out of the place and joined his friend just round the corner. They went so quickly up Bullock Street that I could not catch them."

"Bullock Street," said the detective, and ran up that road as quickly as the strange pair that he was following.

Their journey now took them up narrow, brick ways; streets with few lights and even with few windows. The sun had set further and it was getting dark. It was not easy, even for the London policemen, to guess in what exact direction they were walking. The inspector, however, was almost certain that in the end they would reach some part of Hampstead Heath. Suddenly one gas-lit window broke the half-light. Valentin stopped an instant before a little, brightly-painted sweet shop. After an instant's hesitation he went in. He stood among the bright colours of the shop very seriously and bought some sweets with a certain care. He was clearly making an opportunity to ask some questions. But this was not necessary.

A thin young woman in the shop looked at him without interest; but when she saw the door behind blocked with the figure of the inspector, her eyes seemed to wake up.

"Oh," she said, "if you have come about the parcel, I have sent it off already."

"Parcel?" repeated Valentin.

"I mean the parcel the gentleman left — the priest gentleman."

"Great heavens," said Valentin, leaning forward eagerly, "tell us what happened exactly."

"Well," said the woman, a little doubtfully, "the priests came in about half an hour ago and bought some sweets and talked a bit, and then went off towards the Heath. But a second after, one of them ran back into the shop and said, 'Have I left a parcel?' Well, I looked everywhere and couldn't see one; so he said, 'Never mind; but if you should find it, please post it to this address,' and he left me the address and a shilling for my trouble. And then, though I thought I'd looked everywhere, I found he'd left a brown-paper parcel, so I posted it to the place he said. I can't remember the address now: it was somewhere in Westminster. But as the thing seemed so important, I thought perhaps the police had come about it."

"So they have," said Valentin shortly. "Is Hampstead Heath near here?"

"Straight on for fifteen minutes," said the woman, "and you'll come right out on the open ground." Valentin sprang out of the shop and began to run. The others followed him.

The street that they threaded their way through was so narrow and shut in by shadows that, when they suddenly came out into the open heath and sky, they were surprised to find the evening still so light and clear. As he stood on the slope and looked across the valley, Valentin saw the thing that he was looking for.

Among the black and breaking groups in that distance was one especially black which did not break — a group of two figures dressed like priests. Though they seemed as small as insects, Valentin could see that one of them was much smaller than the other. The other was slightly bent, but he could see that the man was well over six feet high. Valentin went forward, swinging his stick impatiently. By the time he had shortened the distance and made the two figures larger, he noticed something else; something which surprised him, and yet which he had somehow expected. Whoever the tall priest was, there could be no doubt who the other one was. It was his friend of the Harwich train, the short little priest of Essex whom he had warned about his brown-paper parcels.

Now all this was reasonable enough. Valentin had learned by his inquiries that morning that a Father Brown from Essex was bringing up a jewelled silver cross, an ancient object of great value, to show to some of the foreign priests at their meeting in London. This without any doubt was the silver "with blue stones"; and Father Brown was certainly the simple little man on the train. Now there was nothing wonderful about the fact that what Valentin had found out Flambeau had also found out; Flambeau found out everything. Also there was nothing wonderful in the fact that when Flambeau heard of a jewelled cross he should try to steal it; it was the most natural thing in all natural history. And most certainly there was nothing wonderful about the fact that Flambeau should do as he wished with such a foolish sheep as the man with the umbrella and the parcels. It was not surprising that an actor like Flambeau, dressed as another priest, could lead him to Hampstead Heath. So far the crime seemed clear enough; and while the detective pitied the priest for his helplessness, he scorned Flambeau for choosing such a simple, trusting person to deceive. But when Valentin thought of all that had happened in between, of all that had led him here, he could see no reason in it. What had the stealing of a jewelled silver cross from the priest from Essex to do with throwing soup at walls? What had it to do with calling nuts oranges, or with paying for windows first and breaking them afterwards? He had come to the end of his search; yet somehow he had missed the middle of it. He had found the criminal, but still could not understand how it had happened.

The two figures that they followed were moving like black flies across the top of a green hill. They were clearly in deep conversation, and perhaps did not notice where they were going; but they were certainly going to the wilder and more silent heights of the Heath. As the policemen came nearer they had to hide behind trees and even to creep on their hands and knees in deep grass. By these means the hunters even came close enough to the priests to hear the sound of their discussion, but no word could be clearly heard and understood except the word "reason" which was spoken frequently in a high and almost childish voice. Once over a sudden rise in the ground in thick bushes, the detectives actually lost the two figures that they were following. They did not find the right path again for an anxious ten minutes, then it led round the top of a great round hill overlooking a wide hollow of rich, silent sunset scenery. Under a tree in this beautiful yet lonely part of the Heath was an old worn-out seat. On this seat sat the two priests still in serious speech together. The rich colours of green and gold were still to be seen on the darkening horizon; but the hill above was turning from green to dark blue and the stars were appearing in the sky more and more like solid jewels. Valentin made silent signs to his followers and crept up behind a big branching tree, where, scarcely breathing, he heard the words of the strange priests for the first time.

After he had listened for half a minute, he felt a terrible doubt. For the two priests were talking exactly like priests, religiously, with learning and calm. The little Essex priest spoke the more simply, with his round face turned to the brightening stars; the other talked with his head bowed, as if he were not fit to look at them. But no more priest-like conversation could have been heard.

The first he heard was the end of one of Father Brown's sentences, which was: "—— what they really meant in the Middle Ages by the heavens being unchanging and always unspoilt."

The taller priest bowed his head further and said:

"Ah, yes, who can look at those numbers of worlds and not feel that there may well be wonderful universes above us. Yet who knows if in those universes . . . ?"

Valentin behind his tree was tearing his fingernails with

silent anger. He seemed almost to hear the quiet laughter of the English detectives whom he had brought so far on a wild guess only to listen to the talk of two mild old priests. When he listened again, Father Brown was speaking:

"Look at the stars. Don't they look as if they were diamonds and jewels? But don't imagine that all these wonderful things in heaven would make the slightest difference to the reason and justice of one's behaviour. On plains of jewels, under cliffs cut out of pearl, you would still find a notice board, 'Thou shalt not steal.'"

Valentin was just about to rise from his stiff and bent position and to creep away as softly as he could. But something in the silence of the tall priest made him stop until this man spoke. When at last he did speak, he said simply, his head bowed and his hands on his knees:

"Well, I still think that the other worlds may perhaps rise higher than our reason. The mystery of heaven cannot be understood, and I for one can only bend my head."

Then, with his head still bent forward, and without the slightest change in expression, he added:

"Just give me that blue cross of yours, will you? We're all alone here, and I could pull you to pieces like a straw toy."

The completely unchanged voice added a strange violence to that shocking change of speech. But the little priest only seemed to turn his head the smallest degree. He seemed still to have a rather foolish face turned to the stars. Perhaps he had not understood. Or perhaps he understood and sat frozen with fright.

"Yes," said the tall priest, in the same low voice and with his head still bowed, "yes, I am Flambeau."

Then, after a pause, he said:

"Come, will you give me that cross?"

"No," said the other, and the word had a strange sound.

Flambeau suddenly stopped acting like a priest. The great robber leaned back in his seat and laughed quietly for a long time.

"No," he cried, "you won't give it to me, you simple fool. Shall I tell you why you won't give it to me? Because I've got it already in my pocket."

The small man from Essex turned what seemed to be a confused face in the half-light, and said cautiously but eagerly:

"Are — are you sure?"

Flambeau shouted with delight.

"Really, you are amusing!" he cried. "Yes, you fool, I am quite sure. I had the sense to make a copy of the right parcel, and now, my friend, you've got the copy, and I've got the jewels. An old trick, Father Brown — a very old trick."

"Yes," said Father Brown, and passed his hand through his hair in the same strange confused manner. "Yes, I've heard of it before."

The great criminal leaned over to the little country priest with a sort of sudden interest.

"*You* have heard of it?" he asked. "Where have *you* heard of it?"

"Well, I mustn't tell you his name, of course," said the little man simply. "He was a man who had come back to the Church after a life of crime. He lived in wealth and comfort for about twenty years on copies of brown-paper parcels. And so, you see, when I began to suspect you, I thought of this poor man's way of doing it at once."

"Began to suspect me?" repeated the criminal. "Did you really have the sense to suspect me just because I brought you up to this bare part of the Heath?"

"No, no," said Brown, with an expression of apology on his face. "You see, I suspected you when we first met. It's the shape showing in the arm of your coat where you people keep your special weapon."

"How," cried Flambeau, "did you ever hear of this weapon?"

"Oh, one's work, you know!" said Father Brown, "When I was a priest in Hartlepool, there were three people with such weapons. So, as I suspected you from the first I made sure that the cross should be safe, anyhow. I'm afraid I watched you, you know. So at last I saw you change the parcels. Then I changed them back again. And then I left the right one behind."

"Left it behind?" repeated Flambeau, and for the first time there was another note in his voice beside victory.

"Well, it was like this," said the priest, speaking in the same simple way. "I went back to the sweet shop and asked if I'd left a parcel, and gave them a particular address if it was found. Well, I knew that I hadn't; but when I went away again I did. So, instead of running after me with that valuable parcel, they have sent it flying to a friend of mine in Westminster." He added rather sadly: "I learnt that, too, from a poor fellow in Hartlepool. He used to do it with small bags that he stole at railway stations, but he's a good man now. One gets to know, you know," he added rubbing his head with an expression of apology on his face. "We can't help being priests. People come and tell us these things."

Flambeau tore a brown-paper parcel out of his pocket and broke it open. There was nothing but paper and bars of lead inside. He sprang to his feet and cried:

"I don't believe you. I don't believe that a simple fellow like you could manage all that. I believe that you've still got the cross with you, and if you don't give it up — why, we're all alone, and I'll take it by force!"

"No," said Father Brown simply, and stood up also; "you won't take it by force. First, because I really haven't still got it. And, second, because we're not alone."

Flambeau stopped in his step forward.

"Behind that tree," said Father Brown and pointed, "are two strong policemen, and the greatest detective alive. How did they come here, do you ask? Why, I brought them, of course! Lord bless you, we have to know twenty such things when we work among the criminal classes! Well, I wasn't sure you were a thief, and it would not be right to accuse one of our own priests. So I tested you to see if anything would make you show your intentions. A man usually complains if he finds salt in his coffee; if he doesn't he has some reason for keeping quiet. I changed the salt and sugar, and *you* kept quiet. A man generally objects if his bill is three times too big. If he pays it, he has some reason for passing unnoticed. I changed your bill and *you* paid it. Well," went on Father Brown, "as you wouldn't leave any tracks for the police, of course somebody had to. At every place we went to, I took care to do something that would get us talked about for the rest of the day. I didn't do much harm — I dirtied a wall a little, spilt apples, broke a window; but I saved the cross, as the cross will always be saved. It is in Westminster by now."

"How on earth do you know all these things?" cried Flambeau.

The shadow of a smile crossed the round, simple face of Father Brown.

"Oh, by being a simple priest, I suppose," he said, "Have you never thought that a man who does almost nothing except listen to men confessing their crimes is likely to know a little of human evil?"

As he turned to collect his property, the three policemen came out from under the dark trees. Flambeau was an actor and a sportsman. He stepped back and bowed low to Valentin.

"Do not bow to me, my friend," said Valentin in a clear voice. "Let us bow to our master."

And they both stood for a moment with their hats off, while the little Essex priest searched about for his umbrella.

Philomel Cottage
by Agatha Christie

"Goodbye, my love."

"Goodbye, dearest."

Alix Martin leaned over the small garden gate and watched the figure of her husband grow smaller as he walked down the road in the direction of the village.

Soon he turned a bend and disappeared, but Alix still stayed in the same position, with a dreamy, faraway look in her eyes.

Alix Martin was not beautiful. She was not even particularly pretty, but there was a joy and softness in her face which her friends from the past would not have recognised. Alix had not had an easy life. For fifteen years, from the age of eighteen until she was thirty-three, she had had to look after herself (and for seven years of that time her sick mother as well). She had worked as a typist, and she had been neat and business-like. But the struggle for existence had hardened the soft lines of her young face.

It was true that she had had a sort of love affair — with Dick Windyford, a fellow clerk. Although outwardly they had seemed to be just good friends, Alix knew in her heart that he loved her. Dick had worked hard in order to save enough money to send his young brother to a good school. He could not think of marriage yet.

Then suddenly, the girl was delivered from the dullness of her everyday life in the most astonishing manner. A cousin died and left all her money, a few thousand pounds, to Alix. This gave Alix freedom, an easier life and independence. Now she and Dick need wait no longer to be married.

But Dick behaved unusually. He had never spoken directly to Alix of his love for her, and now seemed to have less desire than ever to do so.

He avoided her, and became silent and unhappy. Alix was quick to realise the truth. She had become a wealthy woman, and Dick's pride would not allow him to ask her to be his wife.

She liked him none the worse for it and was, indeed, wondering if she should make the first suggestion, when the second astonishing thing happened to her.

She met Gerald Martin at a friend's house. He fell violently in love with her, and within a week he had asked her to marry him. Alix, who had always considered herself calm and sensible, was completely carried away.

Accidentally she had found a way to excite Dick Windyford. He had come to her hardly able to speak with anger.

"The man's a complete stranger to you! You know nothing about him!"

"I know that I love him."

"How can you know — in a week?"

"It doesn't take everyone eleven years to find out that they're in love with a girl," cried Alix angrily.

His face went white.

"I've loved you ever since I met you. I thought that you felt the same about me."

Alix was truthful.

"I thought so too," she admitted. "But that was because I didn't know what real love was."

Then Dick had burst out again, first with prayers and then with threats — threats against the man who had taken his place. Alix was astonished how strongly the fire burned in the man whom she had thought that she knew so well.

As she leant on the gate of the cottage on this sunny morning, her thoughts went back to that meeting. She had been married for a month, and she was wonderfully happy. Yet now and again there were moments of anxiety which darkened her perfect happiness. And the cause of that anxiety was Dick Windyford. Three times since her marriage she had dreamed the same dream. Although the place was different on each occasion, the main facts were always the same. *She saw her husband lying dead and Dick Windyford standing over him, and she knew quite clearly that it was Dick who had struck him down.*

But if that was terrible, there was something more terrible still, although in the dream it seemed completely natural and expected. *She, Alix Martin, was glad that her husband was dead;* she stretched out grateful hands to the murderer, and sometimes she thanked him. The dream always ended in the same way, with herself held in Dick Windyford's arms.

She had said nothing about this dream to her husband, but secretly it troubled her more than she liked to admit. Was it a warning — a warning against Dick Windyford?

Alix was awakened from her thoughts by the sharp sound of the telephone ringing in the house. She went into the cottage and picked up the receiver. Suddenly she felt faint and put out a hand against the wall.

"Who did you say was speaking?"

"Why, Alix, what's the matter with your voice? I hardly recognised it. It's Dick."

"Oh!" said Alix. "Oh! Where — where are you?"

"At the Traveller's Arms — that's the right name, isn't it? Or don't you even know of the existence of your village inn? I'm on my holiday and doing a bit of fishing here. Would you have any objections if I came to see you both this evening after dinner?"

"No," said Alix sharply. "You mustn't come."

There was a pause, and then Dick's voice, with a slight difference in it, spoke again.

"I beg your pardon," he said formally. "Of course I won't trouble you——"

Alix broke in hastily. He must think that her behaviour was extraordinary. Indeed, it *was* extraordinary. She must be in a bad state of mind.

"I only meant to say that we are — going out tonight," she explained, trying to make her voice sound as natural as possible. "Will you — will you come to dinner tomorrow night?"

But Dick noticed the lack of warmth in her voice.

"Thanks very much," he said in the same formal voice, "but I may leave at any time. I'm expecting to be joined by a friend. Goodbye, Alix." He paused, and then added hastily, with his old friendliness: "Best of luck to you, my dear."

Alix hung up the receiver with a feeling of relief.

"He mustn't come here." she repeated to herself. "He mustn't come here. Oh, what a fool I am to get into a state like this! But even so, I'm glad that he's not coming."

She picked up an old country hat from a table and went out into the garden again, pausing to look up at the name which was cut in the stone above the front door: Philomel Cottage.

"It's a strange name, isn't it?" she had said to Gerald once before they were married. He had laughed.

"You're a funny little girl," he had said lovingly. "I don't believe that you've ever heard a nightingale. I'm glad that you haven't. Nightingales should only sing for lovers. We'll hear them together on a summer's evening outside our own home."

And when Alix, standing in the doorway of their home, remembered how they had indeed heard them, she smiled happily.

It was Gerald who had found Philomel Cottage. He had come to Alix full of excitement about it. He told her that he had found the perfect house for them — a real jewel of a place. And when Alix had seen it she, too, fell in love with it. It was true that it was in rather a lonely position — it was two miles from the nearest village — but the cottage itself was delightful. Its appearance was attractive, and it had a comfortable bathroom, a good hot-water system, electric light and telephone, and Alix was charmed by it immediately. But then they had a great disappointment. Gerald found out that the owner, although a rich man, would not let it. He would only sell.

Gerald Martin had plenty of money, but most of it was in trust and he was unable to use it. He could collect at most a thousand pounds. The owner wanted three thousand. But Alix, who had set her heart on the cottage, came to the rescue. She gave half of her money in order to buy the home. So Philomel Cottage had become their own, and not for a minute had Alix regretted the choice. It was true that servants did not like the loneliness of the country — indeed, at the moment they had none at all — but Alix, who had had little home life before, thoroughly enjoyed cooking delicate little meals and looking after the house. The garden, which was well stocked with the most beautiful flowers, was attended to by an old man from the village who came twice a week.

As she came round the corner of the house. Alix was surprised to see the old gardener busy in the flower beds. She was surprised because his days for work were Mondays and Fridays, and today was Wednesday.

"Why, George, what are you doing here?" she asked, as she came towards him.

"I thought that you'd be surprised, miss. But this is the reason. There's a country show near here on Friday, so I said to myself that neither Mr Martin nor his good wife would mind if I came for once on a Wednesday instead of a Friday."

"That's quite all right," said Alix."I hope that you'll enjoy yourself at the show."

"I intend to," said George simply. "But I did think too, miss, that I'd see you before you go away so as to find out what you want me to do with the flower borders. You haven't any idea when you'll be back, miss, I suppose?"

"But I'm not going away."

George looked at her in astonishment.

"Aren't you going to London tomorrow?"

"No. What gave you such an idea?"

George made a movement with his head over his shoulder.

"I met master going down to the village yesterday. He told me that you were both going away to London tomorrow, and that it was uncertain when you'd be back again."

"Nonsense," said Alix, laughing. "You must have misunderstood him."

Just the same, she wondered exactly what Gerald could have said in order to cause the old man to make such an odd mistake. Going to London? She never wanted to go to London again.

"I hate London," she said suddenly and bitterly.

"Ah!" said George calmly. "I must have been mistaken some-how, and yet he said it quite plainly, it seemed to me. I'm glad that you're staying here. I don't approve of all this moving about, and I don't like London at all. *I've* never needed to go there. Too many motorcars — that's the trouble nowadays. As soon as people have got a motorcar, they can't seem to stay still anywhere. Mr Ames, who used to have this house, was a nice peaceful gentleman until he bought one of those things. He hadn't had it a month before he put up this cottage for sale. He'd spent a lot of money on it, too, putting in electric light and things like that. 'You'll never get your money back,' I said to him. 'But,' he said to me, 'I'll get two thousand pounds for this house.' And he certainly did."

"He got three thousand," said Alix, smiling.

"Two thousand," repeated George. "There was talk at the time about the amount that he wanted."

"It really was three thousand," said Alix.

"Ladies never understand figures." said George firmly. "You're not going to tell me that Mr Ames was bold enough to ask you for three thousand?"

"He didn't ask me," said Alix; "he asked my husband."

George bent down again to his flower bed.

"The price was two thousand," he said with determination.

Alix did not trouble to argue with him. She moved across to one of the further beds and began to pick a bunch of flowers.

As she moved towards the house, Alix noticed a small, dark green object in one of the beds. She stopped and picked it up, recognising it as her husband's notebook of daily events.

She opened it and looked rapidly through it with some amuse-ment. Almost from the beginning of her married life with Gerald, she had realised that, although he was gay and cheerful, he had the unexpected virtues of neatness and organisation. He de-manded that his meals were served on time and always planned his day with great care.

As she looked through the notebook she was amused to notice under the date of May 14th: "Marry Alix St Peter's 2.30." Alix laughed, and turned the pages. Suddenly she stopped.

"'Wednesday, June 18th' — Why that's today."

In the space for that day Gerald had written in his neat, exact hand: "9 p.m." Nothing else. What had Gerald planned to do at 9 p.m.? Alix wondered. She smiled to herself as she realised that, if this had been a story like those which she had read so often, the notebook would have contained some unpleasant surprise. It would have had in it for certain the name of another woman. She turned back the pages carelessly. There were dates, appointments, short references to business deals, but only one woman's name — her own.

But as she slipped the book into her pocket and went on with her flowers to the house, she felt a slight anxiety. She remembered Dick Windyford's words almost as though he had been beside her repeating them: "The man's a complete stranger to you. You know nothing about him."

It was true. What did she know about him? After all, Gerald was forty. In forty years there must have been women in his life
. . . .

Alix shook her head impatiently. She must not think like this. She had a more urgent matter to deal with. Ought she, or ought she not, to tell her husband that Dick Windyford had telephoned her?

It was just possible that Gerald had already met him in the village. But in that case he would be sure to mention it to her immediately upon his return, and she could then safely tell him. Otherwise — what? Alix felt a strong desire to say nothing about it.

If she told him, he was sure to suggest that they invited Dick Windyford to Philomel Cottage. Then she would have to explain that Dick had asked if he could come, and that she had made an excuse to prevent him. And when he asked her why she had done so, what could she say? Tell him her dream? But he would only laugh — or, to make matters worse, he would see that she thought it was important although he did not.

In the end, although she felt rather ashamed, Alix decided to say nothing. It was the first secret that she had ever kept from her husband, and the consciousness of it made her ill at ease.

When she heard Gerald returning from the village at lunchtime, she hurried into the kitchen and pretended to be busy with the cooking so as to hide her confusion.

Alix realised at once that Gerald had not seen Dick Windyford. She was relieved, but she remained a little anxious because she had to prevent Gerald from learning what had happened.

It was not until they had finished their simple evening meal and were sitting in the living room, with the windows open in order to let in the sweet night air and the scent of the flowers, that Alix remembered the notebook.

"Here's something that you've been watering the flowers with," she said, and threw it to him.

"I dropped it in the border, did I?"

"Yes; I know all your secrets now."

"Not guilty," said Gerald, shaking his head.

"What about your secret business at nine o'clock tonight?"

"Oh! that——" He seemed surprised for a moment, then he smiled as though something gave him particular amusement.

"It's a meeting with a specially nice girl, Alix. She's got brown hair and blue eyes and she's very like you."

"I don't understand," said Alix, pretending to be severe. "You're avoiding the point."

"No, I'm not. As a matter of fact, it's a note to remind myself that I'm going to develop some photographs tonight, and I want you to help me."

Gerald Martin was very interested in photography and had an excellent, but rather old, camera. He developed his photographs in the small cellar beneath the cottage, which he had fitted up for that purpose.

"And it must be done at nine o'clock exactly," said Alix, laughing.

Gerald looked a little annoyed.

"My dear girl," he said, with slight anger in his manner, "one should always plan a thing for a certain time. Then one does one's work quickly and properly."

Alix sat for a minute or two in silence, watching her husband. He lay in his chair smoking, with his dark head leaning back and the clear-cut lines of his face showing against the dark background. And suddenly, Alix felt a wave of fright sweep over her, so that she cried out before she could stop herself: "Oh, Gerald, I wish that I knew more about you!"

Her husband looked at her in astonishment.

"But my dear Alix, you do know all about me. I've told you about when I was boy in Northumberland, about my life in South Africa, and about these last ten years in Canada which have brought me success."

"Oh! business!" said Alix scornfully.

"I know what you mean — love affairs. You women are all the same. Nothing interests you but personal things."

Alix felt her throat go dry, as she said without much firmness: "Well, but there must have been — love affairs — if I only knew——"

There was silence again for a minute or two. Gerald Martin looked worried and undecided. When he spoke it was seriously, without any sign of his former light-hearted manner.

"Alix, do you think that it's wise to want to know so much? Yes, there have been women in my life. I don't say that it's not true, and if I did you wouldn't believe me. But I can swear to you truthfully that not one of them was important to me."

His voice was so sincere that Alix was comforted.

"Are you satisfied, Alix?" he asked with a smile. Then he looked at her with curiosity.

"What's made you think of this tonight especially?"

Alix got up and began to walk about the room.

"Oh, I don't know," she said, "For some reason or other I've been feeling anxious all day."

"That's strange," said Gerald in a low voice, as though he was speaking to himself. "That's very strange."

"Why is it strange?"

"Oh, my dear girl, don't turn on me like that. I only said that it was strange because as a rule you're so happy and cheerful."

Alix forced herself to smile.

"Everything's done its best to annoy me today," she confessed. "Even old George had got hold of some extraordinary idea that we were going away to London. He said that you had told him so."

"Where did you see him?" asked Gerald sharply.

"He came to work today instead of Friday."

"The stupid old fool," said Gerald angrily.

Alix looked at him in surprise. Her husband's face was twisted with violent anger. She had never seen him like this. When Gerald saw her astonishment, he made an effort to regain control of himself.

"Well, he is a stupid old fool," he complained.

"What can you have said to make him think that?"

"I? I never said anything. At least — oh, yes, I remember; I made some weak joke about going 'off to London in the morning', and I suppose that he believed me. Or perhaps he didn't hear me properly. You corrected him, of course?"

He waited anxiously for her reply.

"Of course, but he's the sort of old man whom it isn't easy to correct when he's decided on something."

Then she told him how certain George had been about the price of the cottage.

Gerald was silent for a minute or two, then he said slowly: "Ames was willing to take two thousand pounds immediately and to be paid the remaining one thousand in small amounts during several months. That's the origin of that mistake, I expect."

"Very likely," Alix agreed.

Then she looked up at the clock, and pointed to it with a laugh.

"We ought to be getting on with it, Gerald. It's five past nine."

A very odd smile appeared on Gerald Martin's face.

"I've changed my mind," he said quietly. "I shan't do any photography tonight."

A woman's mind is a curious thing. When Alix went to bed on that Wednesday night, her mind was peaceful and contented. Although her happiness had been momentarily in danger, it was now as great as before.

But by the evening of the following day she realised that it was being attacked again. Dick Windyford had not telephoned again, but she felt what she supposed was his influence at work. Again and again she seemed to hear those words of his: *"The man's a complete stranger to you. You know nothing about him."* And with them came the memory of her husband's face and the way that he had said, "Alix, do you think that it's wise to want to know so much?" Why had he said that? There had been a warning in those words. It was as though he had said, "You had better not try to find out about my past life, Alix. You may get an unpleasant shock if you do."

By Friday morning Alix felt certain that there *had* been a woman in Gerald's life — and that he had taken great care to hide the fact from her. Her jealousy, which had formed slowly, now became violent.

Was it a woman that he had been going to meet that night at 9 p.m.? When he had said that he was going to develop photographs, had he been lying?

Three days ago she would have sworn that she knew her husband completely. Now it seemed to her that he was a stranger about whom she knew nothing. She remembered his unreasonable anger against old George, which had been so different from his usual good-tempered manner. Perhaps it was a small thing, but it showed her that she did not really know the man who was her husband.

On Friday afternoon there were several little things that Alix needed from the village. She suggested that she should go and buy them while Gerald remained in the garden; but rather to her surprise he objected strongly to this plan, and stated that he would go himself while she remained at home. Alix was forced to give way to him, but his determination surprised and worried her. Why was he so anxious to prevent her from going to the village?

Suddenly she thought of an explanation which made the whole thing clear. Was it not possible that, although he had said nothing to her, Gerald had, indeed, met Dick Windyford? Her own jealousy had only developed since her marriage. The same thing might have happened with Gerald. He might be anxious to prevent her from seeing Dick Windyford again. This explanation fitted the facts so well, and was so comforting to Alix's troubled mind, that she accepted it eagerly.

But by teatime she was again ill at ease. She was struggling with a temptation that had come to her since Gerald left. At last, after she had told herself repeatedly that she ought to tidy Gerald's dressing room, she went upstairs. She took a duster with her to keep up the pretence that she was just being a good housewife.

"If I was only sure," she repeated to herself. "If I could only be *sure.*"

She tried to believe that Gerald would have destroyed anything to do with a woman in his past life. But the temptation to find out for herself grew stronger and stronger, until at last she could resist it no longer. Although she felt deeply ashamed of herself, she hunted eagerly through packets of letters and papers, searched the drawers and even the pockets of her husband's clothes. Only two drawers escaped her: the lower drawer of the dressing table and the small right-hand drawer of the writing desk were both locked. But Alix had by now forgotten her shame. She was certain that in one of those drawers she would find something connected with this imaginary woman of the past who filled her thoughts.

She remembered that Gerald had left his keys lying carelessly on the table downstairs. She brought them and tried them one by one. The third key fitted the drawer of the writing desk. Alix pulled it open eagerly. There was a chequebook and some money, and at the back of the drawer a packet of letters.

Alix was breathing unsteadily as she untied the ribbon. Then she reddened and dropped the letters back into the drawer, closing and relocking it. The letters were her own, which she had written to Gerald Martin before she married him.

Then she turned to the dressing table. She did not expect to find what she sought, but she wanted to feel that she had not left the search unfinished.

She was annoyed to find that none of the keys in Gerald's bunch fitted this particular drawer. But by now Alix was determined not to be defeated. She went into the other rooms and brought back a collection of keys with her, and found at last that the key of the cupboard in the spare room also fitted the drawers of the dressing table. She unlocked the lower drawer and pulled it open. But there was nothing in it except a roll of old and dirty newspaper cuttings.

Alix breathed more freely again. But even so she looked quickly at the cuttings, because she was curious to know what subject had interested Gerald so much that he had kept them. They were nearly all from American newspapers of about seven years before, and they dealt with the trial of Charles Lemaitre. Charles Lemaitre had been suspected of marrying women in order to murder them for their money. Human bones had been found beneath the floor of one of the houses which he had rented, and most of the women that he had "married" had never been heard of again.

He had defended himself at the trial with the greatest skill, and had been helped by some of the best lawyers in the United States. The court had been unable to prove the main charge of murder, but had found him guilty of several smaller charges, and he had been imprisoned.

Alix remembered the excitement caused by the case, and again some three years later when Lemaitre had escaped from prison. He had never been caught. The English press had discussed at great length the character of the man and his extraordinary power over women, and it had described his excited behaviour in court and his occasional sudden illnesses because of the weak condition of his heart.

There was a picture of him in one of the cuttings and Alix looked closely at it. It showed a thoughtful, bearded gentleman. Who was it that the face reminded her of? Suddenly, with a shock, she realised that it was Gerald himself. The eyes were just like his. Perhaps he had kept the cutting for that reason. She began to read the account beside the picture. It seemed that certain dates had been written in Lemaitre's notebook, and it was suggested that these were the dates on which the women had been murdered. At the trial, a woman stated that Lemaitre had the mark of an old wound on the inside of his left wrist.

Alix dropped the papers and put out a hand to support herself. *On the inside of his left wrist, her husband had the mark of an old wound.*

The room seemed to spin around her. Gerald Martin was Charles Lemaitre! She knew it and accepted it in a flash. Unconnected facts suddenly fitted together like pieces in a puzzle.

The money that had been paid for the house was her money — her money only. Even her dream now had a meaning. In the depths of her mind, although she had never consciously known it, she had always feared Gerald Martin. She had wished to escape from him, and had unconsciously sought Dick Windyford's help. That, too, was why she had accepted the truth so easily, without doubt or hesitation. Lemaitre had meant to kill her too. Very soon, perhaps. . . .

She almost cried out as she remembered something. *Wednesday 9 p.m.* The cellar, with the floor-stones which could be raised so easily! Once before he had buried one of the women that he had murdered in a cellar. It had all been planned for Wednesday night. But was he mad to write down the date and time in his notebook? No. Gerald always wrote down his business appointments: to him, murder was a form of business.

But what had saved her? What could possibly have saved

her? Had he let her off at the last minute? No. In a flash she realised the answer — *old George.*

She understood now her husband's uncontrollable anger. Doubtless he had prepared the way by telling as many people as possible that they were going to London the next day. Then George had come to work when he was not expected. He had mentioned London to her and she had said that the story was untrue. It would have been too risky to murder her that night, if old George was likely to repeat that conversation. But what an escape! If she had not happened to mention that little matter — Alix trembled.

But she had no time to waste. She must get away at once — before he came back. She quickly replaced the roll of cuttings in the drawer, shut it and locked it.

And then she stayed as still as if she had turned into stone. She heard the noise of the gate into the road. *Her husband had returned.*

For a moment Alix remained as though she was frozen, then she crept softly to the window, looking out from behind the shelter of the curtain.

Yes, it was her husband. He was smiling to himself and singing a little song. He held in his hand an object which almost made the frightened girl's heart stop beating. It was a spade.

Alix understood at once. *It was to be tonight* . . . .

But there was still a chance. Gerald, singing his little song, went round to the back of the house.

She didn't hesitate for a moment. She ran down the stairs and out of the cottage. But just as she came out of the front door, her husband reappeared round the other side of the house.

"Hullo," he said, "where are you running off to in such a hurry?"

Alix did her best to remain as calm as usual. Her chance had gone for the moment but it would come again later, if she took care not to make him suspicious. Even now, perhaps. . . .

"I was going to walk to the end of the road and back." she said in a voice which seemed to her weak and uncertain.

"All right," said Gerald, "I'll come with you."

"No, please, Gerald. I'm not feeling too well — I'd rather go alone."

He looked at her attentively. She thought that a momentary suspicion shone in his eyes.

"What's the matter with you, Alix? You're pale, and you're shaking."

"Nothing." She forced herself to smile and sound confident. "I've got a headache, that's all. A walk will do me good."

"Well, you can't say that you don't want me," said Gerald, laughing. "I'm coming, whether you want me or not."

She dare not object any more. If he suspected that she *knew*. . . .

With an effort she regained most of her usual manner. But she had an uncomfortable feeling that he looked at her sideways every now and then, as if his suspicions were still not completely calmed.

When they returned to the house he made her lie down, and cared for her like any tender husband. Alix felt as helpless as if she was in a trap with her hands and feet bound.

He would not leave her alone for a minute. He went with her to the kitchen and helped her to bring in the simple cold dishes which she had already prepared. She knew now that she was fighting for her life. She was alone with this man, help was miles away and she was absolutely at his mercy. Her only chance was to calm his suspicions so that he would leave her alone long enough for her to reach the telephone in the hall and call for help. That was her only hope now.

She had a momentary flash of hope as she remembered how he had given up his plan before. She was on the point of telling him that Dick Windyford was coming up to see them that evening, but she realised that this would be useless. This man would not be stopped a second time. There was determination in his calm behaviour that made her feel sick. He would simply murder her immediately and calmly telephone Dick Windyford with a story that they had been called away suddenly. Oh! if Dick Windyford would come to the house this evening! If Dick . . .

A sudden idea flashed into her mind. She looked quickly sideways at her husband, as though she was afraid that he would understand what was in her mind. Now that she had formed a plan, her courage returned. Her natural manner came back to her completely.

She made the coffee, and they took it outside as they always did when it was a fine evening.

"Oh, yes," said Gerald suddenly, "we'll do those photographs later."

Alix's blood seemed to go cold, but she simply replied, "Can't you manage alone? I'm rather tired tonight."

"It won't take long." He smiled to himself. "And I can promise you that you won't feel tired afterwards."

The words seemed to amuse him. Alix closed her eyes. She had got to carry out her plan now.

"I'm just going to telephone the butcher," she said, quite naturally. "You needn't move."

"To the butcher? At this time of night?"

"Oh, of course his shop's shut, my love. But he's at home all right. Tomorrow is Saturday and I forgot to ask him to bring me some meat for the weekend. The dear old man will do anything for me."

She passed quickly into the house, closing the door behind her. She heard Gerald say, "Don't shut the door." and replied cheerfully, "Are you afraid that I'm going to make love to the butcher, my dear?"

As soon as she was inside, she picked up the telephone receiver and asked for the number of the Traveller's Arms. She was connected immediately.

"Mr Windyford? Is he still there? Can I speak to him?"

Then her heart began to beat more quickly. The door was pushed open and her husband came into the hall.

"Do go away, Gerald," she said angrily. "I hate anyone to listen when I'm telephoning."

He just laughed and sat down.

"Are you sure it's really the butcher that you're telephoning?" he laughed.

Alix was in despair. Her plan had failed. In a minute Dick Windyford would come to the phone. Should she take a risk and cry out for help?

In her anxiety she began to press up and down the little key on the receiver which she was holding, and immediately another plan flashed into her head. When the key was pressed down, the voice could not be heard at the other end, but when it was pushed up, it could.

"It will be difficult," she thought to herself. "I must keep calm, think of the right words and not hesitate for a moment, but I believe that I can do it. I *must* do it."

And at that minute she heard Dick Windyford's voice at the other end of the line.

Alix drew a deep breath. Then she pushed up the key and spoke.

"Mrs Martin speaking — from Philomel Cottage. Please come (she pressed down the key) tomorrow morning with a good cut of beef for two people (she pushed up the key again). *It's very important* (she pressed down the key). Thank you so much, Mr Hexworthy; I hope that you don't mind me ringing up so late, but the meat is really a matter of (she pushed up the key again) *life or death* (she pressed it down). Very well – tomorrow morning (she pushed it up) *as soon as possible."*

She replaced the receiver and turned to face her husband.

"So that's how you talk to your butcher, is it?" said Gerald.

"It's a woman's touch," said Alix.

She was shaking with excitement. He had suspected nothing. Dick would come, even if he didn't understand.

She passed into the sitting room and switched on the light. Gerald followed her.

"You seem to be in very high spirits now," he said, watching her curiously.

"Yes," said Alix, "My headache's gone."

She sat down in her usual seat and smiled at her husband as

he sank into his own chair opposite her. She was saved. It was only twenty-five minutes past eight. Dick would arrive long before nine o'clock.

"I didn't like the coffee that you gave me very much," Gerald complained. "It tasted very bitter."

"It's a new kind that I was trying. We won't have it again if you don't like it, dear."

Alix picked up some sewing. Gerald read a few pages of his book. Then he looked up at the clock and put it away.

"Half past eight. It's time to go down to the cellar and start work."

The sewing slipped from Alix's fingers.

"Oh, not yet. Let's wait until nine o'clock."

"No, my girl — half past eight. That's the time that I arranged. You'll be able to go to bed earlier."

"But I'd rather wait until nine."

"You know that when I arrange a time, I always keep it. Come along, Alix. I'm not going to wait a minute longer."

Alix looked up at him. His hands were shaking and his eyes shining, and he kept on passing his tongue over his dry lips. He no longer tried to hide his eagerness.

Alix thought, "It's true — *he can't wait* — he's like a madman."

He walked over to her, seized her by the shoulder and pulled her to her feet.

"Come on my girl – or I'll carry you there."

He spoke gaily, but there was a fierceness in his voice that was terrible. With a great effort she pushed him away and pressed back against the wall. She was helpless. She couldn't get away — she couldn't do anything — and he was coming towards her.

"Now, Alix——"

"No, no."

She cried aloud, trying hopelessly to keep him away with her hands.

"Gerald — stop — I've got something to tell you, something to confess——"

He did stop.

"To confess?" he said curiously.

"Yes, to confess." She had not chosen those words specially, but she went on despairingly, hoping to hold his attention.

A look of disgust appeared on his face. "A former lover, I suppose?"

"No," said Alix. "Something else. I expect that you'd call it — yes, you'd call it a crime."

At once she saw that she had said the right thing. His attention was held. As soon as she realised this, her courage returned to her. She felt that she was again in charge of the situation.

"You'd better sit down," she said quickly.

She herself crossed the room to her old chair and sat down. She even bent down and picked up her sewing. But behind her calmness she was feverishly inventing a story that would hold his interest until help arrived.

"I told you," she said slowly, "that I had been a typist for fifteen years. That was not entirely true. There were two interruptions. The first was when I was twenty-two. I met a man, a fairly old man, with a little property. He fell in love with me and asked me to marry him. I accepted. We were married." She paused. "I persuaded him to insure his life in my favour."

She saw a sudden look of interest appear on her husband's face, and she went on with increased confidence.

"During the war I worked for a time in a hospital. There I handled all kinds of rare poisons."

There was no doubt that Gerald was extremely interested now. The murderer is bound to have an interest in murder. She had taken a chance on that, and succeeded. She looked quickly at the clock. It was twenty-five minutes to nine.

"There is one poison — it is a little white powder — of which just a tiny amount causes death. You know something about poisons perhaps?"

She put the question with some anxiety. If he did, she would have to be careful.

"No," said Gerald. "I know very little about them."

She was greatly relieved.

"You have heard of the poison which is called hyoscine, of course? The poison that I am speaking of acts in the same sort of way, but afterwards it is impossible to find any sign of it in the body. A doctor would believe that the heart had failed. I stole a small quantity of this poison and kept it."

She stopped.

"Go on," said Gerald.

"No. I'm afraid. I can't tell you. Another time."

"Now," he said impatiently. "I want to hear."

"We'd been married for a month. I was very good to my rather old husband. He praised me to all the neighbours. Everyone knew what a tender wife I was. I always made his coffee myself every evening. One evening, when we were alone together, I put a pinch of the poison in his cup——"

Alix paused, and carefully rethreaded her needle. She had never acted in her life, but at this moment she was the rival of the greatest actress in the world. She was actually living the part of a pitiless poisoner.

"It was very peaceful. I sat watching him. Once he coughed a little and said that he wanted air. I opened the window. Then he said that he could not move from his chair. *In the end he died.*"

She stopped, smiling. It was a quarter to nine. Surely they would come soon.

"How much," said Gerald, "was the money from the insurance?"

"About two thousand pounds. I used it unwisely and lost it. I went back to my office work, but I didn't mean to stay there long. Then I met another man. He didn't know that I'd been married before. He was a younger man, rather good-looking, and he had a little money. We were married quietly in Sussex. He didn't want to insure his life, but of course his money was to come to me if he died. He liked me to make his coffee myself just as my first husband had done."

Alix smiled thoughtfully, and added simply, "I make very good coffee."

Then she went on:

"I had several friends in the village where we were living. They were very sorry for me when my husband died suddenly of heart failure one evening after dinner. I didn't really like the doctor. I don't think that he suspected me, but he was certainly very surprised at my husband's sudden death. This time I received about four thousand pounds, and this time I saved it. Then, you see——"

But she was interrupted. Gerald Martin was pointing at her with one shaking hand, and holding his throat with the other.

"The coffee — it was the coffee!"

She looked at him in astonishment.

"I understand now why it was bitter. You devil! You've poisoned me."

His hands seized the arms of the chair. He was ready to spring upon her. Alix stepped back from him to the fireplace. She was thoroughly frightened again. She opened her lips to tell him the truth — and then paused. In another minute he would spring upon her. She gathered all her strength. She looked at him steadily and with command.

"Yes," she said, "I've poisoned you. Already the poison is working. At this moment you can't move from your chair — you can't move——"

If she could keep him there — even for a few minutes.

Ah! what was that? She heard footsteps on the road. She heard the noise of the garden gate. Then footsteps on the path outside, and the outer door opening.

"You can't move," she said again.

Then she slipped past him and rushed from the room to fall, fainting, into Dick Windyford's arms.

"Good heavens! Alix!" he cried.

Then he turned to the man with him, a tall strong policeman.

"Go and see what's happening in that room."

He laid Alix down carefully in a chair and bent over her.

"My little girl," he said softly. "My poor little girl. What have they been doing to you?"

Her eyelids moved once, and her lips just whispered his name.
The policeman returned and touched Dick on the arm.

"There's nothing in that room, sir, except a man sitting in a chair. It looks as if he'd had some kind of bad fright, and——"

"Yes?"

"Well, sir, he's — dead."

They were surprised suddenly to hear Alix's voice.

"And in the end," she said, as if she was in a dream, *"he died."*

The Heel
by Cyril Hare

The police car, which had been called from the county police station at Markhampton, drove quickly around the edge of the American airfield and on up the village street. It was half past eight on a fine spring morning, and the road was empty except for a line of the American army cars that now seemed to be a common sight on the country roads of that particular part of England. Sergeant Place of the Markshire County Police, who was sitting beside the young driver, looked at them with little pleasure. It was not that he had any real objection to Americans. On the whole, they did not behave worse than the local people. But when they did behave badly, the way in which they did so was different. This was, in itself, an offence to Place, who had been brought up to believe in the regular order of things. Consider this business at Hawthorn Cottage, for example — there was sure to be an American mixed up in it, and that would cause trouble.

Hawthorn Cottage was an old, rather dark, little house which stood by itself on the farther side of the village. There were many like it in the area. The owners let them, already furnished, to visiting army officers, and profited greatly by demanding high rents. As the police car reached the entrance, the car of the police doctor came up behind it, and the three men went into the house together.

Sergeant Place was rather relieved when the door was opened by someone who was clearly an Englishman — a middle-aged man with rather unhealthy skin in the dull clothes of a man-servant.

"Will you come this way, please?" he said in the accepted language of his profession, and led them upstairs to the best bedroom. He opened the door and stood aside for them to enter.

The man in the bed had certainly been dead for some hours, because the body was already cold. Sergeant Place judged that he was about forty-five. There was little character in the round face. He was dressed in expensive and rather showy night-clothes, which did not seem to fit the poorly furnished room. On the table by the bed there was a half-empty bottle of spirits, an entirely empty glass, and a small round medicine box which was also empty. On the floor beside the table was a letter with an envelope which was simply addressed, "Mr William Harris". It had not come by post. Place gave some instructions to the young police driver and left the room. He found the servant standing in the passage just outside the door.

"Let's go downstairs, shall we?" he suggested. "We can talk better there."

The man went before him down the narrow staircase into the sitting room. Place watched him closely as he stood, respectful but anxious, in front of the empty fireplace.

"You haven't been here long have you?" he began.

"I — no sir, only three days. We were in London before that. But how——"

"Easy," said Place with a smile. "You forgot to lower your head for the beam at the top of the stairs. This place was let already furnished, I suppose. To an American?"

"No sir, not to an American. Mr Harris is — was — English. But I understood that he had lived in the United States for some years and, I may say, picked up some American habits."

He was talking more easily now. Place's smile usually made people feel at ease.

"And what's your name?"

"Wilson, sir. Thomas Wilson."

"Well, Wilson, tell me when you found out that your master was dead."

"When I went in this morning to give him his cup of tea, sir. I didn't touch anything, but rang up the police immediately. I hope that I did right."

"Quite right. And when had you last seen him before that?"

"Last night, sir, about 10.30. He'd given me a free evening and when I came in he was just getting into bed."

"And what can you tell me about Mr Harris?"

"I can tell you very little, sir. I had only been with him for two weeks altogether. He hired me through Chiltern's the employment agency. No doubt you've heard of it, sir. But I can tell you that his ways were — well, a little strange, sir."

"Strange? Well, naturally. You've just told me that he had American habits."

"No, sir, I don't mean that they were strange in that way. He was afraid."

"What of?"

"Oh — of people, sir. And of Americans, especially. That was why he took this house. He said that there were too many Americans in London, and that he wanted to get right away from it."

Sergeant Place laughed aloud at the idea of a person coming to Markshire in order to get away from that particular danger.

"He chose the wrong district to come to, then," he said. "Didn't he know that the Americans had a base in the village?"

"It seems that he didn't, sir. I think that it was a great shock to him when he found out. Why, yesterday he said to me——"

Place thought to himself that when you had helped these anxious witnesses to get over their fright, they would wander on for ever. He decided that he had better return to the more important matter. He interrupted Wilson without any apology.

"Do you know anything about this?" he said, and produced the envelope which he had taken from the bedroom.

"That, sir? Oh yes, I gave it to Mr Harris last night when I came in."

"Where did it come from?"

"The staff officer gave it to me to give him."

"I don't understand. What staff officer?"

"I was going to tell you, sir, when you interrupted me," the man said patiently. "It happened yesterday morning. Mr Harris drove down to the village with me to do some shopping and we had to stop in the village street where they are repairing the road. They were letting through only one line of cars at a time. There was an American army car coming the other way. This staff officer was in the front and as he passed he seemed to recognise Mr Harris, sir."

"How did you know that?"

"He spoke to him, sir. Just one word. It sounded like — 'Blimey!'"

"Not a very American word, Wilson. Are you sure it wasn't — 'Limey'?"

"It could have been that, sir. What does that mean, if I might ask?"

"It's a not very polite name for an Englishman. Go on."

"Whatever it was, it seemed to trouble Mr Harris a good deal, sir. He drove on as soon as the car had passed, and never stopped in the village at all. We did our shopping in Markhampton. Then last night I saw the staff officer again."

"Where?"

"At the local inn, sir — the Spotted Dog. I was spending my evening there. The place was full of American soldiers, and he was with them. He recognised me at once and spoke to me. He bought me one or two drinks and then he — well, he began to ask me questions, sir."

"He found out who you were and where you were living and so on?"

"Just so, sir. Then, just before the inn closed, he asked the innkeeper for a bit of paper and an envelope and wrote something and told me to give it to Mr Harris. So I did, sir."

"And you don't know what was written in the letter?"

"Naturally not, sir." In spite of his polite voice, the man was offended. Sergeant Place recognised the expression of blame and smiled slightly.

"You might be interested to know. Here it is." Place read: *"Well, Limey, this is quite a surprise. I'll pay a visit to your little hiding-place about midday tomorrow, so you had better be there."*

"Is that all, sir?"

"That's all. And it's signed — Joe."

"That's the name of the staff officer, no doubt, sir."

"If you saw him again, would you recognise him?"

"All these Americans look very much alike to me, sir, but I dare say I would."

"Well," said Place as he put the letter away, "that appears to be all. You gave him that letter, and he's dead. He died of — what exactly did he die of, doctor?" he asked, as the police doctor came into the room.

"A form of poison, without doubt. I can't say more until we've made a thorough examination. He died about eight to ten hours ago, I should think. I can see no sign of violence. I am going now unless you still want me. Shall I make arrangements to have the body moved?"

"Not just yet, thank you, doctor. I prefer not to have anyone in the house till the afternoon. Perhaps we shall have a visitor about midday."

When he had seen the doctor off, Place called to the young driver, who was upstairs.

"Percy?"

"Yes, Sergeant Place?"

"Take the car round to the back of the house, will you? I don't want it to be seen from the road."

Percy came downstairs.

"I've looked around his room fairly thoroughly," he remarked. "He's got some very showy American clothes. I found this in a drawer: I thought that it might interest you."

He handed to Place a small pile of articles that had been cut from newspapers, and went out to the car. Place saw that the articles were all taken from American papers and were arranged so that the most recent was on top. It was the top one, in fact, that caught his eye. *This morning John Benjamin Spencer was put to death for the murder of bank guard Edward Hart*, it began. He looked through the rest of the articles and found a familiar name. *William S. Harris, who was born in England and was formerly in the same business as the accused, was today called as a witness in the trial of John B. Spencer. . . .*

"Do you need me any more, sir?" said Wilson, who was still in the room.

"No," said Place, whose attention was fixed on the articles. "Yes," he added immediately. "What did Mr Harris do when you gave him the note?"

"He read it, sir."

"Anything else?"

"Then he sent me downstairs to get the bottle of spirits and two glasses."

"Two glasses?"

"Mr Harris was very informal," the man explained. "He had American habits, although he was an Englishman like you or me. He asked me to have a drink with him. He was not at all like any other gentleman that I have served."

Place looked at his unhealthy face and his unsteady fingers, which were stained with tobacco. "You drink quite a lot, don't you, Wilson?" he said.

"A little, sir, I must admit — now and again."

"Is that why you lost your last post?"

"No sir!" He was deeply offended. "I've been in first-class service all my life and my employers have always been pleased with me. My last position was with Lord Gaveston. I was in his Lordship's service for five years, and I only lost that post when he and his wife separated, and the family broke up. This position was not really good enough for me. I accepted it because Chiltern's agency had nothing else to offer at the time, and the wages were good. Chiltern's know me, sir, and they would recommend me for the best employment. Ask them now, if you don't believe me. The telephone number is Belgrave 8290. You can make a long-distance telephone call immediately, if you like."

"I think you've said enough, Wilson. There's no need to get excited." said Place, in order to calm him.

"I'm sorry, sir, but a man in my position depends on a good reputation. I've had a shock and — and I've had no breakfast this morning yet."

"Just finish your story and keep calm. You said that you brought Mr Harris the bottle of spirits. . . ."

"That's right, sir. When I brought it he was sitting on the side of his bed. He poured some of it out into two glasses, and we both had one. Then he told me to leave the bottle and his glass with him and we said good night. I didn't see him again till I found him this morning."

"Thank you, Wilson; you've been most helpful. Now go to the kitchen and get yourself something to eat."

Place looked at his watch. It was just nine o'clock. He had to wait for three hours, if Staff Officer Joe came on time and, indeed, if he chose to come at all. If he did not, it would not be easy to find him. He wondered how many staff officers at the big American base were called Joe. The situation could have been worse, of course. The name on the letter might have been Butch or Red. It appeared to him that half of the American forces were called those extraordinary names. But Joe was nearly as common. Meanwhile, he must wait.

A policeman often has to wait, but this time Place found it quite pleasant. He had a comfortable chair to wait in and a pile of newspaper articles to read. The articles reported a very ordinary kind of murder — a guard had been killed during a bank robbery. And, like many murderers, John B. Spencer looked a very ordinary young man in his photographs. As for Mr Harris, it seemed that he had been lucky only to have been a witness and not on trial with Spencer. Or had he been so lucky? Sergeant Place was not so sure when he thought of the man who had been frightened and was now lying in the bed upstairs. He read the articles again and again until he heard Percy call from the hall, "Here he comes, Sergeant Place!"

Place opened the door for a young man in army dress, who looked at him in surprise.

"Have I come to the right place?" he asked. "They told me that this was Mr Harris's house."

"They told you quite correctly. Come in."

The visitor entered with hesitation. He looked hard at Place, and then at Percy.

"You're policemen, aren't you?" he said, "What's happened?"

"Did you write a letter to Mr Harris last night?"

"I did."

"He was found dead in bed this morning."

The young man took a little time to think this information over. His face showed no expression. As Place watched him, he thought that the line of his jaw seemed familiar.

"Well . . . " he said at last, "that saves a lot of trouble, doesn't it?"

"Does it?" Place asked. "That rather depends on why you wanted to see Mr Harris."

"Perhaps we needn't discuss that at present. I'm grateful that you gentlemen gave me the news, that's all. I'd better go now."

"Wait a minute. Before you go, there are two questions that I'd like to ask you. What sort of man was the late Mr Harris?"

"He was a heel," said the staff officer. "What's the other question?"

"Is your name Spencer, by any chance?"

"Yes, I'm Joseph Wilbur Spencer."

"And John Benjamin Spencer?"

"He was my brother."

"Thank you, Spencer. I think that you have told me all I want to know. Now would you care to see the body and make sure that it is Mr Harris?"

"Sir," said Spencer, "during my stay in this country I have developed a great respect for your police — a very great respect. If you tell me that Harris is dead, I don't ask for any proof. No sir! The word of the British police is good enough for me. But I will say this: you've given me a piece of news that is going to make the people in my home town very thankful when it is known, as certainly it will be. And now I will say good day to you."

"Percy, ask Wilson to come in here for a minute," said Place, after the visitor had gone.

Percy went out to the kitchen, and returned with a smile on his face.

"I think that Wilson has had spirits for breakfast," he said. "I can't wake him up."

"Well — he's had a shock, as he said himself. I don't really need him. We'll ask Scotland Yard to send a man round to Chiltern's. Perhaps they can tell us something about the late Mr Harris. We shall have to find out more than the fact that he was a heel."

He picked up the telephone.

"I want to make a trunk call, please, Miss. Get me——"

He put the instrument down with a crash.

"Percy?" he shouted. "Get the car out, quick, and go after that staff officer. Bring him back at once — by force, if necessary."

To a puzzled and rather annoyed Spencer, Sergeant Place said, "I'm sorry, but I must know for certain if the body upstairs is that of Harris."

"If you say so, sir. I've no real objection to dead bodies, but I should have thought——"

He broke off suddenly as Place threw open the door of the kitchen.

"Limey!" he cried. He bent over the half-conscious figure which was fallen back in a chair, breathing heavily. "They said that you were dead!"

"Not yet," said Place cheerfully. "But he soon will be. There is less delay over British criminal trials than over yours, I fancy. Now, If you don't mind, we'll go upstairs and examine the body of Thomas Wilson – the poor, harmless servant whom Harris poisoned last night, when he got your note. He hoped that when you spread the news of his death he wouldn't be troubled by John Spencer's friends and relatives again. It was a neat plan, and it might have succeeded, if he hadn't forgotten that he was playing the part of an English servant and talked about long-distance telephone calls instead of trunk calls. As he told me himself, he'd picked up a lot of American habits while he was away. I expect that he came down here specially in order to be seen by you and then to pretend to kill himself. Mr Harris was quite a clever criminal."

"Didn't I say that he was a heel?" said Staff Officer Spencer.

The Unlucky Theatre
by Elliott O'Donnell

For many years there was a theatre in London which was regarded as unlucky because for a very long time no play produced in it was a success. It was called The Mohawk, and it had changed its name many times. Originally, at the beginning of the last century, it was called The Cascade. Later, it was known in turn as The Black Hawk, The Beehive, The White Vane and a great many other names, but none of them brought it any good luck. Moreover, people believed that it was visited by ghosts, and this gave it an even worse reputation.

When my old friend Con Fernaghan heard this, he was very eager to spend a night in the theatre. He came from an old Irish family which had, for many centuries, taken an interest in the ways and behaviour of ghosts.

He asked me if I knew who owned the theatre, and I told him that I believed the owner was Peter Lindsey. Lindsey spent a great deal of time abroad, but it so happened that just then he was staying in his house in Chelsea, and Fernaghan soon went to see him. He asked if he could keep watch in the theatre for a night, and Lindsey agreed on condition that he did not tell the newspapers, and that whatever happened was kept a secret. It was arranged that Fernaghan should go to the stage door at eleven o'clock on a Monday night in June, and that he would be admitted when he rang three times. Fernaghan was looking forward eagerly to the night, and at last it arrived. He went to The Mohawk at the correct hour, rang the stage door bell three times, and was let in by the night-watchman, John Ward. On this particular occasion Ward was given a free night, and Fernaghan took his place. Ward showed him round the building, explained to him what to do if there was a fire, and left him alone in the theatre. The place seemed uncomfortably lonely, and after Ward had gone, there was an uneasy stillness, which was broken only by occasional sharp noises such as one hears in old, empty buildings at night. Fernaghan had never imagined that a theatre could be so quiet.

He wandered up and down stairs and along the passages on various floors, looked into the boxes and then went round behind the stage. The dust lay thick on the boards, and there were signs of long neglect everywhere.

Fernaghan was looking at the remains of a large black insect, and hoping that there were no more live ones still about, when he heard a movement in the nearest dressing room. He cautiously opened the door of it and looked in. A man was doing something to a stage sword. When he heard the door open, he turned round and saw Fernaghan. There was a guilty, surprised look in his eyes, and Fernaghan wondered who he was and by what right he was there. Ward had told him that there was nobody in the building. There was something strange about the man. His clothes had long been out of fashion and somehow he did not seem quite real.

"Who are you," Fernaghan asked, "and what are you doing to that sword?"

He took a step towards the man, who suddenly and without explanation melted away. This gave Fernaghan a shock but he gradually calmed himself, and although his thoughts were still rather shaken, he continued to wander round the dusty old place.

When it was nearly one o'clock by his watch he thought that it was time to have something to eat. He had brought some food with him, so he sat below the stage, ate some cold chicken and drank some hot coffee. While he was drinking, he had the feeling that someone was watching him. He looked around him and got such a fright that he almost dropped his cup.

At the edge of the stage was a tall, graceful woman with dark hair and eyes. She was beautiful, but the paleness of her face was striking and decidedly ghostly. She was looking anxiously around the theatre, and when she seemed satisfied that there was no cause for anxiety, she slipped silently across the stage and out of sight.

Now that he had seen two ghosts, Fernaghan thought that he had had enough shocks and that he had better leave The Mohawk, because he certainly did not want to meet a third ghost. But as he did not like to leave anything that he had promised himself to do, he stayed on.

He looked slowly round the theatre. How lonely it seemed! What a feeling of sadness and emptiness surrounded it! There was no sign of life anywhere. He thought of the many feet that had stepped out on the stage, of the attractive faces whose beautiful eyes and smiles had delighted so many people. Where were those well-known actors and actresses now? Probably they were all dead and forgotten.

He leaned back in his seat, closed his eyes and dreamed of the past. Suddenly he heard voices. He opened his eyes, and to his astonishment he was no longer alone in the theatre. The seats were completely filled with people dressed in the fashions of long ago. The house was full but, like the man in the dressing room, these people did not seem real. Their faces were as pale as those of the dead and there was something unpleasantly inhuman about them.

The woman whom Fernaghan had seen on the edge of the stage was now seated alone in a box. She wore a rich evening dress of the kind that might have been worn in the early years of the nineteenth century. She was leaning forward and watching the stage with great attention.

The musicians below the stage were playing an old tune which had once been popular no doubt, but which was now forgotten. They broke off suddenly as the curtain rose. The scene was a wood where two men were about to have a sword fight. One man was tall with fair hair and a beard; the other was dark and had no beard. At a signal from a third man they began to fight.

There was an immediate silence in the theatre, which was broken only by the sharp noises of the fight. Fernaghan looked up at the lady in the box, whose beauty held his attention. She

was watching every sword stroke of the fighters with the greatest anxiety and excitement.

Suddenly the fair man's sword flashed forward and struck the
dark man in the chest. He gave a long cry, took a few unsteady
steps and fell. There was a terrible cry from a girl who had been
watching from behind a stage tree, and a joyful shout from the
lady in the box, who applauded victoriously.

The curtain dropped. In a few moments it rose again, and
Fernaghan was shocked to see a row of skeletons in the clothes
that they had probably worn in the play. The musicians and the
audience were all skeletons and as they applauded with their
bony hands, the actors smiled and bowed and then threw back
their heads and burst into devilish laughter. The curtain fell,
and the theatre was once again in darkness.

Fernaghan couldn't bear any more. He hurried out to the
street.

Peter Lindsey listened to Fernaghan's account of his ghostly
experiences in The Mohawk with great interest, and told him
that they might have been the result of an unfortunate happening
in the theatre in 1803, of which he had once heard a story.

A play called *The Watching Eyes* was being performed at The
Cascade, as The Mohawk was then named. Two leading actors
were in it, Guy Lang and Raymond Ross. Ross was known to be
very much in love with Mrs Lang. She encouraged him and
repeatedly told him that she hated her husband, who treated
her badly.

In the play there was a fight between Lang and Ross, and one
night Ross killed Lang. The stage swords always had rubber
buttons on their points so that no one would be hurt, but on this
occasion the sword used by Ross had no button. It was always
thought that Mrs Lang was responsible and that she intended
her lover, Ross, to kill Lang. It was never known for certain
whether Ross took part in the plan, and as proof of his guilt
could not be found, he was merely dismissed.

Mrs Lang, who was very probably delighted to lose her husband, married Lord Delahoo, whom she had known for some

time. Because of the suspicion of murder that was connected with it, the theatre was closed down and when it opened again it was no longer called The Cascade.

"From that time," Lindsey said, "people claimed that the theatre was visited by ghosts, and no play produced in it was ever a success. It has been a great expense and trouble to me, and if I can't sell it I'll have it pulled down."

But its reputation for ghosts and bad luck was so great that he could not sell it, so he had it pulled down and sold the land on which it had stood.

The Great Idea of Mr Budd
by Dorothy L. Sayers

£500 REWARD

The Evening Messenger is always anxious to see that justice is done. It has therefore decided to offer the above reward to any person who gives information which results in the arrest of William Strickland, also called Bolton. This man is wanted by the police in connection with the murder of Emma Strickland at 59 Acacia Crescent, Manchester.

DESCRIPTION OF THE WANTED MAN

This is the official description of William Strickland: Age forty-three; height about six feet one inch; thick silver-grey hair, which may be dyed; full grey beard, but may now have been shaved off; light grey eyes, set close together; large nose; strong white teeth, of which some are filled with gold, and which are particularly noticeable when he laughs; left thumbnail damaged by a recent blow.

Speaks in rather a loud voice; has quick, decisive manner. May be dressed in a grey or dark blue suit and soft grey hat.

May have left, or be trying to leave, the country.

Mr Budd read the description carefully once again and sadly put the paper to one side. There were hundreds of barbers' shops in London. It was extremely unlikely that William Strickland would choose his small and unsuccessful shop for a haircut, a shave or even to have his hair dyed. And Mr Budd did not suppose that he was in London, in any case.

Three weeks had passed since the murder, and it seemed very probable that William Strickland had already left the country. But in spite of this Mr Budd memorised the description as well as possible. There was a chance — just a small chance — as there had been with the many competitions which he had entered. These were difficult times for Mr Budd, and he was attracted by any opportunity of making money.

It may seem strange that, in an age when it was fashionable for ladies to have their hair treated, Mr Budd should search for opportunities of making money. But recently a new "Ladies Hairdressing Department" had opened opposite, with attractive and well-dressed young hairdressers, two rows of shining new wash basins, purple and orange curtains and a large electric sign with a red border.

The result was an endless stream of young ladies who hurried there to make appointments. If they were forced to wait for three or four days, they did not think of crossing the road to Mr Budd's poorly-lighted shop. Day after day, Mr Budd watched them going in and out of the rival shop and prayed in a rather uncertain way that some of them would come over to him; but they never did.

And yet Mr Budd knew that he was the finer artist. Sometimes he felt sad when he watched ladies coming out of the shop opposite, and saw how poorly their hair had been done. He knew that he could have done it better for them. But Mr Budd had studied especially the art of hair-dyeing, and it made him quite angry to see the careless way in which his rival did this particular branch of his work.

Yet nobody came to Mr Budd except workmen and a few people who happened to be passing.

Why did Mr Budd not modernise his shop also and make it bright, clean and attractive? The reason is simple and unfortunate. Mr Budd had a younger brother, Richard, and had promised his mother that he would look after him. In those days, he had owned an excellent business in his home town of

Northampton, and Richard had been a bank clerk. Richard had got into bad ways (poor Mr Budd blamed himself very much for this). He had lost nearly all his money, and tried to put things right by taking the bank's money. But Richard was not nearly skilful enough to escape with it, and he had been sent to prison. Mr Budd repaid the bank and the people to whom Richard owed money. And when Richard came out of prison he gave him and his wife tickets to Australia and enough money for them to begin a new life there.

But this took all the profits from his hairdressing business. He also felt that he couldn't stay in Northampton, where people had known him since he was a boy. So he had come to the great city of London and bought this little shop. He had done fairly well until the new business had opened on the other side of the road.

That is why Mr Budd searched the newspaper every morning for opportunities of making money.

He put the newspaper down and, as he did so, caught sight of his face in the glass and smiled, because he was still able to make fun of himself. He was not the sort of man who catches a violent murderer by himself. He was well into middle age and was five feet six inches tall at the most. Moreover, he was getting rather fat and beginning to lose his hair.

Even with a razor, he would be no match for William Strickland, height about six feet one inch, who had murdered his old aunt so violently, cut her body in pieces and buried her remains in the garden. Mr Budd shook his head doubtfully and walked towards the door to watch the busy shop opposite. As he did so he nearly ran into a large man who suddenly came in through the doorway.

"I beg your pardon, sir," said Mr Budd politely, not wanting to lose ninepence. "I was just stepping outside for a breath of fresh air, sir. Would you like a shave sir?"

The large man quickly took off his coat without waiting for Mr Budd's help.

"Are you ready to die?" he asked fiercely.

The question fitted in with Mr Budd's thoughts about murder

so closely that for a moment he was quite frightened.

"I beg your pardon, sir," he managed to say at last, and in the same moment decided that the man must be a preacher of some kind. He looked rather like it, with his strange, light eyes, his thick red hair and the short beard which stuck out from his chin. Perhaps he was going to demand money. That would be a pity, because Mr Budd had been looking forward to ninepence or, with a tip, possibly even a shilling.

"Do you dye hair?" said the man impatiently.

"Oh!" said Mr Budd, feeling relieved, "yes, sir, certainly, sir."

This was a stroke of luck. He could charge as much as seven shillings and sixpence for dyeing.

"Good," said the man, sitting down and allowing Mr Budd to put a cloth about his neck. "The fact of the matter is that my young lady doesn't like red hair. She says that it attracts too much attention. The other young ladies in her office make jokes about it. She's a good deal younger than I am, you see, so I like to please her, and I thought that perhaps it could be changed to something less noticeable. Dark brown is the colour that she would like. What do *you* think?"

Mr Budd thought that the young ladies might consider this sudden change even funnier than the original colour, but in the interests of business he agreed that dark brown would be very nice and a great deal less noticeable than red. Besides, it was very likely that there was no young lady. A woman, he knew, would say that she wanted her hair to be a different colour for a change or because she thought that it would make her hair look nice. But when a man is going to do something foolish he prefers, if possible, to put the responsibility on to someone else.

"Very well, then," said the man, "carry on. And I'm afraid that the beard must go. My young lady doesn't like beards."

"A great many young ladies don't, sir," said Mr Budd. "Beards aren't as fashionable now as they used to be. Luckily, sir, I don't think that it will matter with you. You have a good-looking chin, sir."

"Do you think so?" said the man, examining himself in the

glass a little anxiously. "I'm very glad to hear it." He sat back and laughed, and Mr Budd noticed with approval strong, well-kept teeth, one of which was filled with gold. Clearly this was a man who was ready to spend money on his personal appearance. Mr Budd imagined this wealthy gentleman returning regularly and telling his friends about him. Hair-dyeing was difficult. He must not allow anything to go wrong.

"I see that you have used a dye before, sir," said Mr Budd, with respect. "Could you tell me——?"

"Eh?" said the man. "Oh, yes — well the fact is, as I said, that my young lady is a good deal younger than I am. I expect you can see that my hair began to go grey early in my life — it was the same with my father and all my family — and so I had the grey patches recoloured. But she doesn't really like the colour, so I thought that if I have to have my hair dyed I would change it to a colour she does like, eh?"

It is a common joke, among people who do not think, that barbers talk too much. This is the barber's wisdom. He hears many secrets and very many lies, but he learns to keep them to himself while he talks cheerfully about the weather and politics.

So Mr Budd spoke lightly of the extraordinary behaviour of a woman's mind while he examined the man's hair with trained eye and fingers. And he soon saw that this hair could never — never — have been red. It was naturally black hair which had turned early to a silvery grey. But that was not his business. He got from the man the name of the dye which had been used formerly and noted that he would have to be careful. Some dyes do not mix well with other dyes.

Mr Budd talked pleasantly as he shaved off the offending beard. He washed the hair, as was necessary before he could put the dye on, and then began to dry it. Meanwhile, he talked about sport and politics, and passed on naturally to the Manchester murder.

"The police seem to have given up in despair," said the man.

"Perhaps the reward will help," said Mr Budd who, not surprisingly, was still thinking of that subject.

"Oh, there's a reward, is there? I hadn't seen that."

"It's in this evening's paper, sir. Would you like to have a look at it?"

"Thanks, yes, I would."

Mr Budd fetched *The Evening Messenger*. The stranger read the article carefully and Mr Budd, watching him in the glass, saw him suddenly pull back his left hand, which was resting carelessly on the arm of the chair. But not before Mr Budd had seen it. Not before he had seen the misshapen thumbnail. Mr Budd told himself hurriedly that many people had such an ugly mark. His friend, Bert Webber, had cut off the top of his thumb in an accident with his motorcycle, and his nail looked very much like that.

The man looked up sharply and Mr Budd saw his eyes watching him closely in the glass. It was a terrible warning that the man was examining Mr Budd's reflection to find out how much he knew.

"But I've no doubt," said Mr Budd, "that the man is safely out of the country by now. They've offered the reward too late, I think."

The man laughed.

"I think they have," he said. Mr Budd wondered whether many men who had a damaged left thumb also had an upper tooth filled with gold. There were probably hundreds of people like that in the country, and they probably also had silver-grey hair ("which may be dyed") and were about forty-three years old. Without doubt, Mr Budd thought to himself.

He finished drying the man's head and began to comb the hair which nature had never, never made such a deep red.

He remembered, with an exactness which frightened him, the number and extent of the violent wounds suffered by the old lady in Manchester. Mr Budd looked quickly through the door and noticed that his rival across the street had closed. The streets were full of people. How easy it would be . . .

"Be as quick as you can, won't you?" said the man pleasantly, but a little impatiently. "It's getting late. I'm afraid that I'll keep you over time."

"Not at all, sir," said Mr Budd. "It doesn't matter in the least."

No — if he tried to rush out of the door, this terrible man would jump on him, drag him back and break his head open as he had done to his aunt.

But Mr Budd was certainly in a position of advantage. A determined man would be out in the street before the man could get out of the chair. Mr Budd began to move round cautiously towards the door.

"What's the matter?" said the man.

"I was just stepping outside to look at the time, sir," said Mr Budd, pausing obediently. (But he could have done it then, if he had had the courage to take the first quick step that would make his intentions clear.)

"It's twenty-five minutes past eight," said the man. "I'll pay extra for keeping you late."

"Certainly not, sir," said Mr Budd. It was too late now. He couldn't make another attempt. He imagined himself falling over the doormat and saw in his mind the terrible hand raised to beat him to death. Or perhaps, under the familiar white cloth, the misshaped hand was actually holding a gun.

Mr Budd went to the back of his shop, collecting his materials for dyeing. If he had been quicker — more like a character in a book — he would have realised sooner what that thumbnail and that tooth meant. He would have run out for help while the man's head was wet and soapy, and his face was buried in the towel. Or he could have put soap in his eyes — nobody could murder you or even run away down the street if his eyes were full of soap.

Even now, was it really too late? He could take a razor, go up quietly behind the unsuspecting man and say in a firm, loud voice: "William Strickland, put up your hands. Your life is in my hands. Stand up until I take your gun away. Now walk straight out to the nearest policeman." But Mr Budd couldn't seriously believe that the attempt would succeed. Because if he held the razor to the man's throat and said: "Put up your hands," the man would probably seize him by the wrist and take the razor away. Or what was he to do if he said to the man: "Put up your hands," and the man said "I won't"? He could not remain there with his razor at the man's throat until the boy came in the morning to clean out the shop.

Mr Budd told himself that he didn't have to arrest the man. "Information which results in the arrest" — those were the words. He would be able to tell them that William Strickland had been in his shop, that he no longer had a beard and that his hair was now dark brown. He might even follow him when he left — he might—

It was at this moment that Mr Budd had his Great Idea.

As he fetched a bottle from the glass-fronted case, he remembered with great clearness, an old wooden paper-knife that had belonged to his mother. On the handle had been painted the words "Knowledge is Power".

Mr Budd experienced a strange feeling of freedom and confidence. He picked up the razors with easy, natural movements, and made light conversation as he skilfully dyed the man's hair dark brown.

The streets were less crowded when Mr Budd let him out. He watched the tall figure cross the square and get onto a number 24 bus.

"But he was only being clever," said Mr Budd as he put on his hat and coat, and turned out the lights carefully. "He'll change to another bus which is going in a different direction."

He closed the door of the shop and shook it, to make sure that he had locked it properly. Then he, too, crossed the square and caught a number 24 bus.

The policeman at Scotland Yard didn't take Mr Budd seriously at first when he demanded to see "somebody very important". But when the little barber continued so earnestly to say that he had information about the Manchester murder, and that there was no time to waste, he allowed him to pass through.

Mr Budd told his story first to an important-looking officer, who listened very politely and made him repeat very carefully the bits about the tooth which was filled with gold, the thumbnail and the hair which had been black before it was grey or red and which was now dark brown.

The officer then rang a bell and said, "Perkins, I think that Sir Andrew would like to see this gentleman at once." Mr Budd was taken to another room where there was an even more important-looking man. This one listened to his story with even greater attention and called in another officer to listen too. They wrote down the exact description of the man who was, without doubt, William Strickland.

"But there's one more thing," said Mr Budd. "I hope, sir, I really do hope that it's the right man, because if it isn't my reputation will be ruined——"

He crushed his soft hat into a ball as he leaned across the table and explained the Great Idea that he had had.

"Tzee—z-z-z—tzee—tzee—z-z—tzee—z-z——."
"Dzoo—dz-dz-dz—dzoo—dz—dzoo—dzoo—dz——."
"Tzee—z—z."

The fingers of the radio officer on the ship *Miranda*, which was on the way to Ostend, moved quickly as they wrote down the messages of the busy, noisy radio.

One of them made him laugh.

"The captain had better have this, I suppose," he said.

The captain scratched his head when he read it, and rang a little bell to call the first officer. The first officer ran to the second officer, who picked up the passenger list and went away. The bell was rung again — this time to call the third officer.

"Tzee—z-z—tzee—z-z-z—tzee—tzee—z—tzee."

The message flashed to ships all round the coast of Britain, and in every ship the captain sent for the first officer, and the first officer sent for the second officer. It flashed to harbours and police centres in England, France, Holland, Germany, Denmark and Norway, and the people in them who were able to understand heard, with laughter and excitement, the story of Mr Budd's Great Idea.

The *Miranda* reached Ostend at 7 a.m. A man burst into the cabin where the radio officer was just finishing his work.

"Here!" he cried; "you're to send this message. Something's happening, and the Captain's sent for the police."

The officer turned to his radio. "Tzee—z—tzee——" A message started on its way to the English police.

"Man described by police is on board. Ticket bought in name of Watson. Has locked himself in cabin and refuses to come out. Is demanding that a hairdresser is sent to him. We have been in touch with Ostend police. Waiting for orders."

An excited group of people had collected in front of first-class cabin number 36, and the captain had to give some sharp commands before he could clear a way for himself. He ordered them to leave, and at last only he and five sailors were guarding the cabin. In the silence, the passenger in number 36 could be heard walking up and down the narrow cabin, moving things and knocking them over.

Soon they heard steps above them. Somebody arrived with a message. The captain read it and made a sign. Silently, six Belgian policemen came down the stairs.

"Are you ready?"

"Yes."

The captain knocked at the door of number 36.

"Who is it?" cried a hard, sharp voice.

"The hairdresser that you sent for is here, sir."

"Ah!" The voice was full of relief. "Send him in alone, please, I — I have had an accident."

"Yes, sir."

At the sound of the lock being turned, the captain stepped forward. The door opened a little and was quickly pushed to again, but the captain had stuck his shoe between it and the doorpost. The policemen rushed forward. There was a shout and a shot, which went harmlessly through the window, and the passenger was brought out.

"Good heavens!" shouted the cabin boy. "Good heavens! He's gone green in the night."

Green!

Mr Budd had not wasted the years which he had spent studying the behaviour of dyes. "Knowledge is Power." The knowledge of Mr Budd had given him the power to put a mark on his man which made him different from every other person in the world. A murderer could hide himself nowhere when every hair on his head was bright green.

Mr Budd got his five hundred pounds. *The Evening Messenger* printed the full story of his Great Idea. But Mr Budd was a little afraid. Surely no-one would ever come to him again.

On the next morning a large blue car rolled up Wilton Street and stopped outside his door. A lady, wearing many jewels and an expensive fur coat, swept into the little shop.

"You *are* Mr Budd, aren't you?" she cried. "The *great* Mr Budd? I think that you're *quite* wonderful. And now, *dear* Mr Budd, you *must* do me a favour. You must dye my hair green, *at once. Now.* I want to be able to say that I'm the *first* to be done by you. I'm the Duchess of Winchester and Lady Melcaster is following me down the street, because *she* wants to be the first — she's a cat!"

If you want it done, I can give you the number of Mr Budd's well-known rooms which are in the most fashionable part of London. But I understand that it's extremely expensive.

The Mezzotint
by M. R. James

The London art dealer J. W. Britnell is well known to those with
even the most limited interest in the type of picture which
represents particular places. He sends out regularly excellent
lists of a large and ever-changing collection of prints, plans and
old drawings of country houses, churches and towns in England
and Wales. These lists were, of course, the basis of his subject to
Mr Williams, whose work was to add to his university's collection of English prints and drawings, which was already better
than any other. But because his collection was so large,
Mr Williams bought regularly rather than in great quantity. He
expected Mr Britnell to fill up the less important gaps rather
than to supply him with rare works.

Now, in February of last year a list from Mr Britnell appeared
on Mr Williams's desk, and with it a letter from the dealer
himself. This letter read as follows:

> Dear Sir,
> We beg to call your attention to No. 978 in the
> enclosed list, which we shall be glad to send for
> your examination.
>
> > Yours faithfully,
> > J. W. Britnell

When Mr Williams turned to No. 978 he found the following
description:

> 978 *Unknown*. Interesting Mezzotint: View of a
> country house, early part of the last century.
> 15 by 10 inches; black frame.   £2 2s.

It was not specially exciting, and the price seemed high. However, as Mr Britnell, who knew his business, seemed to think

well of it, Mr Williams wrote a postcard asking for the picture to be sent for him to see, together with some other prints and drawings which appeared in the same list. And so he passed, without much excitement or expectation, to the ordinary work of the day.

A parcel of any kind always arrives a day later than you expect it and that from Mr Britnell was no exception. It was delivered to Mr Williams's office by the afternoon post of Saturday, but after he had left the office. A servant, therefore, brought it round to his rooms in college so that he would not have to wait until Monday for an opportunity to examine the contents and return what he did not propose to keep. And here he found it when he came in to tea with a friend.

The only object with which I am concerned was the rather large, black-framed mezzotint that was described in Mr Britnell's list. It was not of a high quality, and a mezzotint which is not of a high quality is, perhaps, the worst sort of print there is. It presented a full-face view of a not very large country house of the eighteenth century. The house had three rows of plain windows, surrounded by rough stone, a low, ornamental wall with stone balls set at the angles, and a small, covered entrance in the centre. There were trees on either side, and in front there was a large space of well-cut grass. The words "A. W. F. *sculpsit**"* were cut on the narrow edge of the picture, but no other words appeared on it. The whole thing gave one the feeling that it was the work of a not very skilled person. Mr Williams could not imagine why Mr Britnell was demanding £2 2s. for such an object. He turned it over with a good deal of scorn. On the back was a piece of paper, the left-hand half of which had been torn off. Only the ends of two lines of writing remained: the first had the letters *-ngley Hall*; the second, *-ssex.*

Mr Williams thought that it would be just worth the trouble to find out where the place was that was represented, and this he

---

* *sculpsit:* A Latin word. Here it means 'made (this picture)'.

could do easily with the help of a map. He would then return the picture to Mr Britnell with some sharp remarks about the judgment of that gentleman.

When the lamps were alight, because it was now dark, and the tea made, the friend — let us call him Dr Binks — took up the framed print and said:

"What's this place, Williams?"

"That's just what I'm going to try to find out," said Williams, as he went to the shelf for a map. "Look at the back. Something-ley Hall, in either Sussex or Essex. Half the name has gone, you see. You don't happen to know it, I suppose?"

"It's from that man Britnell, I suppose, isn't it?" said Binks. "Is it for the collection?"

"Well, I think that I should buy it if the price was five shillings," said Williams; "but for some extraordinary reason he wants over two pounds for it. I can't imagine why. It's a miserable print and there aren't even any figures to give life to it."

"I certainly don't think it's worth as much as that," said Binks; "and yet I don't think it's so badly done. The moonlight seems rather good to me; and it looks to me as if there are figures, or at least a figure, just on the edge in front."

"Let's look," said Williams. "Well, it's true that the sense of light is rather cleverly brought out. Where's your figure? Oh, yes! Just the head in the very front of the picture."

And indeed, although it was little more than a black spot on the extreme edge of the print, there was the head of a man or a woman. It was well wrapped up, its back was turned and it was looking towards the house.

Williams had not noticed it before.

"But even so," he said, "though it's more skilfully done than I thought at first, I can't spend over two pounds of the university's money on a picture of a place I don't know."

Doctor Binks, who had work to do, soon went, and Williams spent the remaining time before dinner in vain attempts to find out the name of the Hall in the picture. "If the vowel before the *ng* had been left, there would have been no difficulty," he thought; "but as it is, the name may be anything from Guestingley to Langley. There are many more names that end in -ngley than I thought; and this useless book doesn't provide a list of endings."

Dinner in Mr Williams's college was at seven o'clock, but we do not need to know what happened during the meal. Later in the evening, he returned with some friends to his rooms where, doubtless, they played cards and smoked tobacco. After some time, Williams picked up the mezzotint from the table. He did not look at it, but handed it to a person mildly interested in art, and told him where it had come from and the other details which we already know.

The gentleman took it without great excitement, looked at it and then said, in a voice of some interest:

"It's really a very good piece of work, Williams; it has quite an imaginative quality. The light is excellently controlled, it seems to me, and the figure, though it's rather strange, is somehow very striking."

"Yes, isn't it?" said Williams, who was just then pouring out drinks for his other friends and was unable to come across the room to look at the view again.

It was by this time rather late in the evening, and the visitors were beginning to leave. After they had gone, Williams had to write one or two letters and finish some pieces of work. At last, a short time after midnight, he was ready to go to bed and lit a small lamp to take to his bedroom. The picture lay with the face upwards on the table where the last man who had looked at it had put it, and Williams caught sight of it as he put out the sitting room lamp. He declares now, in fact, that if he had been left in the dark at that moment he might have fainted with fright. But, as that did not happen, he was able to steady himself and take a good look at the picture. It was absolutely certain — quite impossible, no doubt, but absolutely certain. In the middle of the well-cut grass in front of the unknown house there was a figure where no figure had been at five o'clock that afternoon. It was creeping on hands and knees towards the house, and it was wrapped in strange, black clothing with a white cross on the back.

I do not know what is the right thing to do in a situation of this kind. I can only tell you what Mr Williams did. He took the picture by one corner and carried it across the passage to a second set of rooms which he possessed. There he locked it up in a drawer, fastened the doors of both sets of rooms, and went to bed; but first he wrote out and signed an account of the extraordinary change that had happened in the picture since he had had it.

Sleep came to him rather late; but he was comforted to know that he was not the only witness of the behaviour of the picture. Clearly, the man who had looked at the mezzotint earlier that night had seen the same sort of thing that he himself had seen. Otherwise he might have been tempted to believe that something seriously wrong was happening either to his eyes or to his mind. As this was fortunately impossible, there were two things he must do in the morning. He must ask a second person to act as a witness and examine the picture with him, and he must make a determined effort to find out the house that was represented in it. He would therefore invite his neighbour, Nisbet, to have breakfast with him, and then he would study the map for the rest of the morning.

Nisbet was free, and arrived about 9.30. I am sorry to say that his host was not quite dressed, even at this late hour. During breakfast, Williams said nothing about the mezzotint, except that he had a picture about which he wished to have Nisbet's opinion. Those who are familiar with university life can easily imagine the delightful conversation of two Fellows of Canterbury College during a Sunday morning breakfast. Yet I am forced to say that Williams found it difficult to be attentive. His interest was naturally centred on that very strange picture which was now lying, face downwards, in the drawer in the opposite room.

At last breakfast was finished, and he was able to light his pipe. The moment had arrived for which he had been waiting. His excitement was so great that he was almost trembling. He ran across and unlocked the drawer, then took out the picture — still face downwards — ran back and put it into Nisbet's hands.

"Now," he said, "Nisbet, I want you to tell me exactly what you see in that picture. Describe it in detail, if you don't mind. I'll tell you why in a moment."

"Well," said Nisbet, "I have here a view of a country house — English, I believe — by moonlight."

"Moonlight? Are you sure of that?"

"Certainly. It seems to be past the full moon, if you wish for details, and there are clouds in the sky."

"All right. Go on. I'll swear," added Williams to himself, "that there was no moon when I saw it first."

"Well, there isn't much more to be said," Nisbet continued. "The house has one — two — three rows of windows, and there are five windows in each row except at the bottom where there's a covered entrance instead of the middle one, and——"

"But what about figures?" said Williams with marked interest.

"There aren't any," said Nisbet; "but——"

"What! There is no figure on the grass in front?"

"Not a thing."

"You'll swear to that?"

"Certainly. But there's just one other thing."

"What?"

"Why, one of the windows on the ground floor — to the left of the door — is open."

"Is it really? Good heavens! he must have got in," said Williams with great excitement. He hurried to the back of the chair on which Nisbet was sitting and seized the picture from him to make sure of the matter for himself.

It was quite true. There was no figure, but there was an open window. For a moment Williams was so surprised that he could not speak. Then he went to the writing table and wrote hastily for a short time. When he had finished he brought two papers to Nisbet. He asked him to sign the first one, which was the description of the picture that you have just read. And he asked him to read the second one, which was the description that Williams had written the night before.

"What does it all mean?" said Nisbet.

"Exactly," said Williams. "Well, there is one thing that I must do — or rather there are three things. First, I must find out what Garwood, who looked at the picture last night, saw. Secondly, I must photograph the thing before it changes further. And thirdly, I must find out where the house is."

"I can photograph it myself," said Nisbet, "and I will. But, you know, I feel as if we were watching some terrible event being worked out somewhere. The question is, has it happened already, or is it about to happen? You must find out where the place is." He looked at the picture again. "Yes," he said, "I expect that you're right: he has got in. And I feel sure that something unpleasant is going to happen in one of the rooms upstairs."

"I've got an idea," said Williams. "I'll take the picture across to old Green." (Green was the oldest Fellow of the college, and had managed its business for many years.) "He'll probably know where the house is. The college has property in Essex and Sussex, and he must have travelled a great deal in those parts of England."

"Yes, he probably will know where it is," said Nisbet; "but just let me take my photograph first. But look here, I don't think that Green is here today. He wasn't at dinner last night, and I think I heard him say that he would be away on Sunday."

"Yes, that's true," said Williams. "I know that he's gone to Brighton. Well, if you'll take the photograph now, I'll go across to Garwood and get his description. Meanwhile you must continue to watch it. I'm beginning to think that two pounds is not such a high price for it after all."

In a short time he had returned and brought Mr Garwood with him. Garwood said that when he had seen the figure it was no longer at the edge of the picture, but that it was not far across the grass. He remembered that the figure had had a white mark on the back of its clothing, but he was not sure if it had been a cross. All this was written down and signed, and Nisbet then photographed the picture.

"Now what do you mean to do?" he said. "Are you going to sit down and watch it all day?"

"Well no, I don't think so," said Williams. "I rather imagine that we are intended to see the whole thing. You see, between the time that I saw it last night and this morning, there was time for a lot of things to happen, but the figure has only reached the house. In that time, it could have done its business easily and gone away again. But as the window is open, I think that it must be inside now. So I feel confident that we can leave it. And, besides, I have an idea that the picture won't change much, if at all, in the daytime. We could go for a walk this afternoon and come in to tea when it gets dark. I shall leave it on the table here, and lock the door. Then, only my servant can get in."

The three men agreed that this would be a good plan; and so we may leave them alone until five o'clock.

At or near that hour the three returned to Williams's rooms. They were slightly annoyed at first to see that the door of his rooms was unlocked; but they quickly remembered that on Sunday the college servants came for their orders earlier than on weekdays. But a surprise was waiting for them. First, they saw that the picture was leaning against a pile of books on the table, as it had been left. The next thing that they saw was Williams's servant, Robert who was sitting on a chair opposite and looking at it with fear in his eyes. Why was this? Robert had a reputation for his excellent manners. He would never sit down on his master's chair or appear to take any particular interest in his master's furniture or pictures. Indeed, he seemed to feel this himself. He sprang up quickly when the three men entered the room and said:

"I beg your pardon, sir. I shouldn't have sat down."

"It doesn't matter, Robert," answered Mr Williams. "I was meaning to ask you for your opinion of that picture."

"Well, sir, I don't compare my opinion with yours, but I

wouldn't hang that picture where my little girl could see it."

"Wouldn't you, Robert? Why not?"

"No, sir. Why, I remember that once the poor child saw a book with pictures not nearly so bad as that one there, and we had to sit up with her for three or four nights after that. And if she saw this evil spirit, or whatever it is that is carrying off the poor baby, she would be in a terrible state. You know what children are like. But what I say is that it doesn't seem the right picture to leave about, sir. If anybody saw it accidentally, he might have an unpleasant shock. Do you want anything else this evening, sir? Thank you, sir."

With these words the excellent man left to visit the rest of his masters. The three gentlemen immediately gathered round the mezzotint. There was the house, as before, under the clouds and the moon that was no longer full. The window that had been open was shut, and the figure was once more on the grass. But this time it was not creeping cautiously on hands and knees. Now it stood up straight and was marching quickly, with long steps, towards the front of the picture. The moon was behind it, and the black clothing hung down over its face so that hardly anything of it could be seen. Indeed, the little of it that could be seen made the three gentlemen deeply thankful that they could see no more than the upper part of its face and a few irregular hairs. The head was bent down, and the arms were tightly closed over an object which could just be seen and recognised as a child. It was not possible to say whether it was dead or living. Only the legs of the figure could be seen plainly, and they were terribly thin.

Between five and seven o'clock the three companions sat and watched the picture in turn. But it never changed. They agreed at last that it would be safe to leave it, and that they would return after dinner and wait for further happenings.

They met again as soon as possible. The print was there, but the figure had gone, and the house was quiet in the moonlight. So now they must search through the maps and guidebooks until they found out where the house was. Williams was the lucky person in the end, and perhaps he deserved to be. At 11.30 p.m. he read the following lines from Murray's *Guide to Essex*:

$16\frac{1}{2}$ miles. *Anningley*, The church was originally an interesting building of the twelfth century, but it was greatly changed in the eighteenth century. It contains the graves of the family of Francis whose seventeenth-century country house, Anningley Hall, stands just beyond the churchyard in a large park. The family has now died out. The last son was lost mysteriously in childhood in the year 1802. The father, Mr Arthur Francis, was known in the district as quite a good artist in mezzotint. After the loss of his son, he lived entirely alone at the Hall, and was found dead in his room exactly three years later. He had just completed a mezzotint of the house, copies of which are extremely rare.

This seemed to be the end of the search and, indeed, when Mr Green returned to the college be immediately recognised the house as Anningley Hall.

"Is there any kind of explanation of the figure?" Williams asked him.

"I really don't know, Williams. I knew Anningley before I came to this university and there used to be one or two stories about Arthur Francis. He was always very severe with any man whom he suspected of stealing or killing animals on his land. Gradually he got rid of all such thieves with the exception of one man, who was called Gawdy, I believe. Gawdy was the last member of a very old family which, it was said, had once been the most important family in the area. He could claim that the graves of his fathers were inside the church and not out in the churchyard like those of common people, and he felt a good deal of bitterness that his family had lost its former greatness. And so, from jealousy of the family of Francis, he began to steal from it with great skill; and it was said that Francis could never prove anything against him. At last, however, the keepers of Francis's lands caught him in a wood on the extreme edge of the park. I could show you the place even now, because it is right beside some land that used to belong to my uncle. As you can imagine, there was a fight, and this man Gawdy most unluckily shot one of the keepers. Well, that was just what Francis wanted. There was a hasty and most unsatisfactory trial, and poor Gawdy was hanged as quickly as possible. I've been shown the place where he was buried. It's on the north side of the church where they buried any person who had been hanged or who had killed himself. The poor fellow had no relatives because he was the last member of his family, but people believed that some friend of his must have planned to seize Francis's boy in order to put an end to *his* family, too. But, you know, although it's an extra-ordinary thing for an Essex thief to think of, I should say now that it looks as if old Gawdy had managed the thing himself. Ugh! I hate to think of it! Have a drink, Williams!"

I have only to add that the picture is now in the Ashleian Collection. It has been tested in order to find out whether the artist used a special kind of ink which could account for its strange behaviour, but without any result. Mr Britnell knew nothing about it except that he was sure that it was an uncom-mon picture. And although it was watched with great care, it has never been known to change again.

Family Affair
by Margery Allingham

The newspapers were calling the McGills' house in Chestnut Grove "the *Mary Celeste* house" before Chief Inspector Charles Luke noticed that the two mysteries were alike. He was so shaken that he telephoned Albert Campion and asked him to come over.

They met in the Sun, a quiet little inn in the High Street, and discussed the case in the small public room which, at that time of day, was empty.

"The two stories *are* alike," Luke said as he picked up his drink. He was a dark, tough and very active man; and as usual he was talking continuously, using his hands to add force to his words: "I'd almost forgotten the *Mary Celeste* mystery, but I read a fresh report of it in the *Morning News* today. Of course, the *Mary Celeste* was a ship, and 29 Chestnut Grove is an ordinary, unexciting little house, but otherwise the two stories are nearly the same. There was even a half-eaten breakfast left on the table in both of them. It's very strange, Campion."

Campion, who was quiet and fair and wore glasses, listened attentively as his habit was. And, as usual, he looked hesitant and a little uncertain of himself; a great many men had failed to regard him seriously until it was too late. At the moment he appeared to be mildly amused. He was always entertained by the force of Luke's excitement.

"You think that you know what has happened to Mr and Mrs McGill, then?" he asked.

"Good heavens, no!" The policeman opened his small, black eyes to their widest. "I tell you that it's the same story as the mystery of the *Mary Celeste*. They've simply disappeared. One minute they were having breakfast together like every other married pair for miles around, and the next minute they had gone without a sign."

Mr Campion hesitated. He looked rather self-conscious. "As I remember the story of the *Mary Celeste* it had the simple charm of being completely unbelievable," he said at last. "Consider it: a band of quite ordinary-looking sailors brought a ship called the *Mary Celeste* into Gibraltar, and had a wonderful story to tell. They said that she was found in mid-ocean with all her sails set, but without a single person on board. The details were astonishing. There were three cups of tea on the captain's table and they were still warm. In his room there was a box of female clothes which were small enough to be a child's. A cat was asleep in the kitchen, and in a pot on the stove was a chicken ready to be cooked." Campion let out a long breath. "Quite beautiful," he said, "but witnesses also swore that with no one at the wheel she was still on her course. The court of inquiry found that too much to believe, although they discussed it for as long as they could."

Luke looked at him sharply.

"That wasn't what the *Morning News* suggested this morning," he said. "They called it 'the world's favourite unsolved mystery'."

"So it is!" Mr Campion was laughing. "Because nobody wants an ordinary explanation which uncovers dishonesty and greed. The mystery of the *Mary Celeste* is an excellent example of the story which really is a bit too good to spoil, don't you think?"

"I don't know. I hadn't thought of it." Luke sounded slightly annoyed. "I was just telling you the main outlines of the two events — 1872 and the *Mary Celeste* is rather too long ago for me. But 29 Chestnut Grove is certainly my business, and I'm not allowing any witness to use his imagination in this inquiry. Just give your attention to the facts and details, Campion."

Luke put down his glass.

"Consider the McGills," he said. "They seem ordinary, sensible people. Peter McGill was twenty-eight and his wife Maureen was a year younger. They had been married for three years and got along well together. For the first two years they had to live with his mother, while they were waiting for the right kind of house to come into the market. But they weren't very happy there, so they rented two rooms from Maureen's married sister. Then after six months this house in Chestnut Grove was offered to them."

"Did they have any money troubles?" Mr Campion asked.

"No." Luke clearly thought that this was an extraordinary fact. "Peter seems to be the one member of the family who had nothing to complain about. He works in the office of a company of locksmiths in Aldgate, and they are very pleased with him. He has a reputation for not spending more than he can afford and, in any case, his wages were raised recently. I saw his employer this morning and he was really anxious, poor old boy. He liked the young man and had nothing but praise for him."

"What about Mrs McGill?"

"She's another good type. She's steady and careful, and she remained at work until a few months ago when her husband decided that she should retire in order to enjoy the new house and raise a family. She certainly did her housework well. The place is still in excellent order although it has been empty for six weeks."

For the first time Mr Campion's eyes became alive with interest. "Forgive me," he said, "but do the police usually enter a case of missing persons so quickly? What are you looking for, Charles? A body? Or bodies?"

"Not officially," Luke said. "But I can't help wondering what we shall find. We came into the case quickly because we heard about it quickly. The situation was unusual and the family were rather frightened. That's the explanation of that." He paused for a moment. "Come along and have a look at the house. We'll come back and have another drink after you've seen it, but this is something that's really special, and I want your help."

Mr Campion followed him out into the network of neat little streets which ran between rows of box-shaped houses set in neat little flower gardens.

"We go down to the end and along to the right," Luke said as he pointed towards the end of the avenue. "I'll tell you the rest of the story as we go. On June 12th, Bertram Heskith, who is the husband of Maureen's elder sister and lives in the next-but-one house, dropped in to see them as he usually did just before eight o'clock in the morning. He came in at the back door, which was open, and found a half-eaten breakfast for two on the table in the bright new kitchen. No one was about, so he sat down to wait."

Luke's long hands were busily forming the scene in the air as he talked, and Mr Campion felt that he could almost see the little room with its inexpensive but not unattractive furniture and the pot of flowers at the window.

"Bertram is a toy salesman and one of a large family," Luke went on. "He's got no work at the moment but he's not unhappy about it. He talks rather a lot, he's grown a little too big for his clothes and he enjoys a drink, but he's got a sharp mind — too sharp, I would say. He would have noticed anything unusual at once. But, in fact, the tea in the pot was still warm, so he poured himself a cup, picked up the newspaper which was lying open on the floor by Peter McGill's chair and started to read it. After a time, he realised that the house was very quiet so he went and shouted up the stairs. As there was no reply he went up and found that the bed was unmade, that the bathroom was still warm and wet with steam, and that Maureen's everyday hat, coat and handbag were lying on a chair. Bertram came down, examined the rest of the house, then went out into the garden. Maureen had been doing some washing before breakfast and the clothes on the line were almost dry. Otherwise, the little square of land was quite empty." He gave Campion a quick look out of the corner of his eye. "And that, my boy, is all," he said. "Neither Peter nor Maureen has been seen since. As they didn't appear again, Bertram told the rest of the family and, after two days, went to the police."

"Really?" Campion showed an unwilling interest. "Is that *all* that you know?"

"Not quite, but the rest of the information is hardly helpful." Luke sounded almost pleased. "Wherever they are, they're not in the house or garden. If they walked out, no one saw them; and they would need both skill and luck for that, because they were surrounded by interested relatives and friends. The only things that anyone is sure that they took with them are two clean sheets. 'A fine pair of sheets' one lady called them."

Mr Campion raised his eyebrows in surprise.

"That's a delicate touch." he said. "I suppose that there is no sign of any crime?"

"Crime is really becoming quite common in London. I don't know what's happening to the old place," Luke said sorrowfully. "But this household seemed healthy and happy enough. The McGills appear to have been ordinary, pleasant young people, and yet there are one or two little things that make one wonder. As far as we can find out, Peter did not catch his usual train to work, but we have one witness — a third cousin of his — who says that she followed him up the street from his house to the corner just as she did every morning during the week. At the top of the street she went in one direction and she thought that he went in the other as usual. But no one else seems to have seen him and she's probably mistaken. Well, now, here we are. Stand here for a minute."

He had paused on the path of a narrow street, shaded by trees and lined with pairs of pleasant little houses of a kind which is now a little out of fashion.

"The next house along here belongs to the Heskiths," he went on, lowering his voice. "We'll walk rather quickly past it because we don't want any more help from Bertram at the moment. He's a good fellow but he believes that Maureen's property is in his trust, and the way in which he follows me around makes me feel self-conscious. His house is number 25, and 29 is next but one. Now number 31, which is actually joined to 29 on the other side, is closed. The old lady who owns it is in hospital; but in 33 live two sisters who are aunts of Peter's. They moved there soon after him and Maureen.

"One is a widow, and the other is unmarried, but they are both very interested in the nephew and his wife. The widow is quite kindly towards her young relatives, but her unmarried sister, Miss Dove, is rather critical of them. She told me that Maureen was careless with money, and I think that from time to time she had had a few words with the girl on the subject. I heard about 'the fine pair of sheets' from her. I believe that she had told Maureen she shouldn't have bought something so expensive, but Maureen had saved up a long time for them."

Luke laughed. "Women are like that." he said. "They get a desire for something, and they make sure that they have it. Miss Dove says that she watched Maureen hanging out the sheets on the line early in the morning of the day that she disappeared. She has an upstairs window in her house from which she can just see part of the garden of 29 — if she stands on a chair."

He smiled. "She happened to be doing that at about half past six on the day that the McGills disappeared, and she is quite sure that she saw them hanging on the line — the sheets, I mean. She recognised them by the pattern on the top edge. They're certainly not in the house now. Miss Dove suggests delicately that I should search Bertram's house for them!"

Mr Campion looked thoughtful, though his mouth was smiling.

"It's quite a story," he said quietly. "The whole thing just can't have happened. How very strange, Charles. Did anybody else see Maureen that morning? Could she have walked out of the front door and come up the street with the sheets over her arm and not have been noticed? I'm not asking if she *would* have done so, but if she *could.*"

"No," said Luke decidedly. "Even if she had wanted to do so, which is unlikely, it's almost impossible. There are the cousins opposite, you see. They live over there in the house with the red flowers, directly in front of number 29. It is one of them who says that she followed Peter up the road that morning. Also there's an old Irish grandmother who sits up in bed in the window of the front room all day. You can't completely trust what she says — for example, she can't remember if Peter came out of the house at his usual time that day — but she would have noticed if Maureen had come out. No one saw Maureen that morning except Miss Dove who, as I told you, watched her hanging the sheets on the line. The newspaper comes early. The milkman heard her washing machine when he left his bottles at the back door, but he did not see her."

"What about the postman?"

"He can't help. He hasn't been doing this work for very long and can't even remember if he called at 29. It's a long street and, as he says, the houses are all alike. He gets to 29 about 7.25 and doesn't often meet anybody at that hour. He wouldn't recognise the McGills if he saw them, in any case. Come on in, Campion – look around and see what you think."

Mr Campion followed his friend up a narrow garden path. A police officer stood on guard at the front door. Mr Campion looked back over his shoulder just in time to see a movement behind the curtains in the house opposite. Then a tall, thin woman, whose face bore no expression, walked down the path of the next house but one and bowed to Luke as she paused at her gate before going back.

"Miss Dove," said Luke unnecessarily, as he opened the door of number 29 Chestnut Grove.

The house had few surprises for Mr Campion. It was almost exactly as he had imagined it. There was not very much furniture in the hall and front room, but the kitchen-dining room was clearly used a great deal and possessed a character of its own. Someone without much money, but who liked nice things, had lived there. He or she — and he thought that it was probably she — had been generous, too, in spite of her efforts to save up, because he noticed little things which had clearly been bought at the door from beggars. The breakfast table had been left exactly as Bertram Heskith had found it, and his cup was still there.

Campion wandered through the house without saying anything, and Luke followed him. The scene was just as he had been told. There was no sign of packing, hurry or violence. A set of man's night-clothes was on the chair in the bathroom, and a towel hung over the edge of the basin to dry. The woman's coat and handbag were on a chair in the bedroom and contained the usual mixture of things and also two pounds, three shillings and a few pennies, and a set of keys.

Mr Campion looked at everything – the clothes hanging neatly in the cupboards, and even the dead flowers which were still in their pots. But the only thing which seemed to interest him was a photograph, taken at Peter and Maureen's marriage, which he found in a silver frame on the dressing table.

Although it was a very ordinary picture, he stood before it for a long time in deep thought. As sometimes happens, the two figures in the centre attracted less attention than the rest of the group of guests, who were laughing cheerfully. Maureen, with her graceful figure and big dark eyes, looked gentle and a little frightened, and Peter, although solid and with a determined chin, had an expression of anxiety on his face which compared strangely with Bertram Heskith's confident smile.

"You can see what sort of a fellow Bertram is," said Luke. "You wouldn't call him a gentleman, but he's not a man who imagines things. When he says that he felt the two had been in the house that morning, as safe and happy as usual, I believe him."

"Miss Dove isn't here?" said Campion, still looking at the group in the photograph.

"No. Her sister is there, though. And that's the girl from the house opposite, who thinks that she saw Peter go up the road."

Luke pointed to the face of another girl. "There's another sister here and the rest are cousins. I understand that the picture doesn't do justice to Maureen's prettiness. Everybody says that she was a very pretty girl. . . ." He corrected himself, "Is, I mean."

"Peter looks a reasonable type to me," said Mr Campion, "although a little uncomfortable, perhaps."

"I wonder." Luke spoke thoughtfully. "The Heskiths had another photo of him and in that there was a kind of hardness and determination in the face. In the war I knew an officer with a face like that. Generally, he was quite a mild man, but when something excited him, he behaved with great firmness. But that's unimportant. Come and examine the clothesline and then you'll know as much as I do."

Luke led the way to the back and stood for a moment on the stone path, which ran under the kitchen window and separated the house from the small square of grass which formed the garden.

On the right, the garden was separated from the neighbouring gardens by a fence and a line of bushes. On the left, the plants in the neglected garden of the old lady who was in hospital had grown up so high that one was sheltered from the eyes of everyone except Miss Dove. Mr Campion supposed that, at that moment, she was standing on her chair to watch them. At the bottom there were a garden hut and a few fruit trees.

Luke pointed to the empty line which hung above the grass. "I brought in the washing," he said. "The Heskiths were afraid that it would decay, and there seemed no reason to leave it outside."

"What's in the hut?"

"A spade, a fork and a machine to cut the grass," said Luke promptly. "Come and look. The floor is made of beaten earth and it has clearly not been dup up for years. I suppose that we'll have to dig it up in the end, but it will be a waste of time."

Mr Campion went over and looked into the wooden hut. It was tidy and dusty, and the floor was dry and hard. Outside, an old ladder leaned against the high brick wall at the end of the garden.

Mr Campion carefully tried the strength of the old ladder. It supported his weight, so he climbed up and looked over the wall. There was a narrow path between the wall and the fence of the back garden of the house in the next street.

"That's an old path that leads down between the two roads," Luke said. "This isn't really a very friendly district, you know. The people in Chestnut Grove think that they're of a better class than the people in Philpott Avenue, which is the road on the other side of the path."

Mr Campion got down from the ladder. He was smiling and his eyes were bright.

"I wonder if anybody in Philpott Avenue noticed her," he said, "She must have been carrying the sheets."

Luke turned round slowly and looked at him in astonishment.

"Are you suggesting that she simply walked down the garden and over the wall and out? In the clothes in which she'd been washing? It's mad. Why should she do it? And did her husband go with her?"

"No, I think that he went down Chestnut Grove as usual and turned back down this path as soon as he came to the other end of it near the station. Then he picked up his wife, and went off with her through Philpott Avenue to catch the bus. They only needed to go as far as Broadway in order to find a taxi."

Luke was still completely in the dark.

"But *why*?" he demanded. "Why should they disappear in the middle of breakfast on a Monday morning? And why should they take the sheets? Young married people can do the most unlikely things — but there are limits to them, Campion! They didn't take their savings books, you know. There isn't much in them but they're still in the writing desk in the front room. What are you suggesting, Campion?"

Campion walked slowly back to the square of grass.

"I expect that the sheets were dry and that she'd put them into the clothes basket before breakfast," he began slowly. "As she ran out of the house, she saw them lying there and couldn't resist taking them with her. The husband must have been annoyed with her, but people are like that. When they're running away from a fire, they save the strangest things."

"But she wasn't running away from a fire."

"Wasn't she!" Mr Campion laughed. "Listen, Charles. If the postman called, he reached the house at 7.25. I think that he did call and that he delivered a plain brown envelope which was so ordinary that he couldn't remember it. Now, who was due at 7.30?"

"Bertram Heskith. I told you."

"Exactly. So there were five minutes in which to escape. Five minutes for a determined and practical man like Peter McGill to act promptly. Remember, his wife was generous, and she was not the sort of person to argue. And so, because of his decisive nature, Peter seized his opportunity.

"He had only five minutes, Charles, in which to escape from all those people whose cheerful, greedy faces we saw in the photograph. They all lived extraordinarily close to him — they surrounded him, in fact — and it wasn't easy to leave unseen. He went out by the front door so that the watchful eyes would see him as usual and not be suspicious.

"There wasn't time to take anything with them. But, as Maureen ran through the garden to escape by the back way, she saw the sheets in the basket and couldn't resist her treasures, so she took them with her. She wasn't quite as hard as Peter. She wanted to take something from their past life, although the promise of a new life was so bright. . . ."

Campion broke off suddenly. Chief Inspector Luke, who had begun to understand, was already moving towards the gate on his way to the nearest police telephone box.

Mr Campion was at home in Bottle Street, Piccadilly, that evening when Luke called. The Chief Inspector came in cheerfully, and seemed very amused.

"It was the Irish Sweep, not the football pools, that they won," he said. "I got the details from the men who organise it. They've been wondering what to do since they read the story in the newspapers. They're in touch with the McGills, of course, but Peter has taken great care to keep his good fortune secret. He must have known that his wife had a generous nature, and decided what he would do if he had a really big win. As soon as he got the letter which told him of his luck, he put his plan into action."

Luke paused and shook his head in admiration. "I can understand why he did it," he said. "Seventy-five thousand pounds is more than plenty for two people, but not very much if it is shared amongst a very big family."

"What will you do?"

"The police? Oh, officially, we are completely puzzled, and in the end we shall drop the matter. It's not our business — it's strictly a family affair."

He sat down and took the drink that his host handed to him. "Well, that's the end of the *Mary Celeste* house," he said. "I was completely fooled by it. I just didn't understand it. But good luck to the McGills! You know, Campion, you were right when you said that an unsolved mystery is only unsolved because no one wants to spoil it. How did you guess the solution?"

"The charm of relatives who call at seven thirty in the morning makes me suspicious," said Mr Campion.

The Invisible Man
by G. K. Chesterton

In the cool blue of the late evening, at the corner of two steep streets in Camden Town in London, a young man of not less than twenty-four was looking into the window of a cake and sweet shop. He was a tall, strong, red-haired young man, with a determined face. His name was John Turnbull Angus. For him this shop had an attraction, but this attraction was not completely explained by the cakes and sweets in the window.

He entered at last, and walked through the shop into the back room, which was a sort of tea-room. He merely raised his hat to the young lady who was serving there. She was a dark, neat girl in black, with very quick dark eyes. After a short pause she followed him into the back room to write down his order.

His order was clearly a usual one. "I want, please," he said, "one halfpenny cake and a small cup of black coffee." An instant before the girl turned away he added, "Also, I want you to marry me."

The young lady of the shop stiffened suddenly, and said, "Those are jokes I don't allow."

The red-haired man lifted his grey eyes and said, "Really and truly, I am serious."

The dark young lady had not taken her eyes off him and seemed to be studying him closely. Then, with a slight smile on her face she sat down in a chair.

"Don't you think," remarked Angus, "that it's rather cruel to eat these halfpenny cakes? They might grow up into penny cakes. I shall give up these cruel sports when we are married, Laura."

The dark lady rose from her chair and walked to the window, clearly in a state of strong but not unsympathetic thought. At last she swung round, returned to her chair, put her arms on the table and looked at the young man not unfavourably, but with a little annoyance.

"You don't give me time to think," she said.

"I'm not such a fool," he answered.

She was looking at him; but she had grown more serious behind the smile.

"Before there is a minute more of this nonsense," she said steadily, "I must tell you something about myself as shortly as I can."

"Delighted," replied Angus.

"It's nothing that I'm ashamed of, and there isn't anything that I'm specially sorry about. But what would you say if there were something which is not my fault and yet troubles me like a bad dream?"

"In that case," said the man seriously, "I should suggest that you bring me another cake."

"Well you must listen to the story first," said Laura. "To begin with, I must tell you that my father owned the inn called the Red Fish at Ludbury, and I used to serve people there. Ludbury is a sleepy, grassy little place in eastern England. Half the people who came to the Red Fish were occasional commerical travellers. The rest were the most unpleasant people you can see, only you never see them. I mean little, lazy men who had just enough to live on, and nothing to do but lean about in the inn, in clothes that were just too good for them. Even these poor characters were not very common in our inn; but there were two of them that were a lot too common. They both lived on money of their own, and were extremely idle and dressed in very bad taste. But yet I was a bit sorry for them, because I half believed they crept into our little empty inn because each of them was rather ugly; with the sort of ugliness which unsympathetic people laugh at. One of them was surprisingly small. He had a round black head and a neat black beard, and bright eyes like a bird's; he wore a great gold watch chain; and he never came into the inn except dressed just too much like a gentleman to be one. He was not a fool, though he never did any work. He was strangely clever at all kinds of things that couldn't be the slightest use. He was always playing tricks with matches, or cutting toys out of fruit and making them dance. His name was Isidore Smythe; I can see him now, with his little dark face, amusing us in the inn.

"The other fellow was more silent and more ordinary. But somehow he frightened me much more than poor little Smythe. He was very tall and thin, and light-haired. He might almost have been good-looking but he had the most terrible squint I have ever seen or heard of. When he looked straight at you, you didn't know where you were yourself, and you certainly didn't know what he was looking at. I fancy this squint made the poor fellow a little unfriendly towards the world. For while Smythe was ready to show off his tricks anywhere, James Welkin (the man with the squint) never did anything except drink in the inn, and go for walks in the flat, grey country all round. All the same I think that Smythe was a little self-conscious about being so small, though he hid it quite successfully. And so I was really puzzled, as well as surprised, and very sorry, when they both offered to marry me in the same week.

"Well, I did what I've since thought was perhaps a foolish thing. But these men were my friends in a way; and I was frightened that they would think I refused them for the real reason, which was that they were so extremely ugly. So I made up some nonsense of another sort, and said that I never meant to marry anyone who had not made his fortune in the world by his own efforts. I said that I could not live on money like theirs which had not been earned. Two days after I had talked like this, the whole trouble began. The first thing that I heard was that both of them had gone off to make their fortunes.

"Well, I've never seen either of them from that day to this. But I've had two letters from the little man called Smythe, and really they were rather exciting."

"Ever heard of the other man?" asked Angus.

"No, he never wrote," said the girl, after an instant's hesitation.

"Smythe's first letter was simply to say that he had started out to walk with Welkin to London; but Welkin was such a good walker that the little man dropped behind, and took a rest by the side of the road. He happened to be picked up by some travelling show, and partly because he was so very small, and partly because he was really clever at his tricks, he got on well in the show business. That was his first letter. His second was much more surprising, and I only got it last week."

The man called Angus emptied his coffee cup and looked at her with mild and patient eyes. Her own mouth had a slight smile on it as she went on: "I suppose that you've seen the advertisements about this 'Smythe's Silent Service'? Or you must be the only person who hasn't. Oh, I don't know much about it. It's some clockwork invention for doing all the house-work by machinery. You know the sort of thing: 'Press a button — A servant who never drinks.' 'Turn a handle — ten servants who never eat.' You *must* have seen the advertisements. Well, whatever these machines are, they are earning a great deal of money; and they are earning it all for that little man whom I knew down in Ludbury. I can't help feeling pleased that the poor little fellow is a success; but the plain fact is that I am frightened that he will arrive at any minute and tell me that he has made his fortune — as he certainly has."

"And the other man?" asked Angus quietly.

Laura Hope got to her feet suddenly. "I haven't seen a line of the other man's writing and I haven't the slightest idea of what or where he is. But it is of him that I am frightened. He seems to be everywhere. It is he that has nearly driven me mad. Indeed, I think he *has* driven me mad; for I've felt him where he couldn't have been, and I've heard his voice when he couldn't have spoken."

"Well, my dear," said the young man cheerfully, "if he were the devil himself, he is defeated now that you have told somebody. One goes mad all alone. But when was it you imagined that you felt and heard our friend with the squint?"

"I heard James Welkin laugh as plainly as I hear you speak," said the girl, steadily. "There was nobody there, for I stood just outside the shop at the corner, and could see down both streets at once. I had forgotten how he laughed, though his laugh was as strange as his squint. I had not thought of him for nearly a year. But it's a solemn truth that a few seconds later the first letter came from his rival."

"Did you ever make this invisible man speak or anything?" asked Angus, with some interest.

Laura trembled, and then went on in a steady voice: "Yes. Just when I had finished reading the second letter from Isidore Smythe, which told of his success, I heard Welkin say: 'But he shan't have you.' It was quite plain, as if he were in the room. It is terrible; I think I must be mad."

"If you were really mad," said the young man, "you would think that you were not. But certainly there seems to be something a little extraordinary about this invisible gentleman. If you would allow me as a practical man——"

Even as he spoke, there was a sort of roar in the street outside, and a small motorcar, driven at wild speed, arrived at the door of the shop and stopped there. In the same flash of time a little man in a tall, shiny hat stood in the outer room.

Angus, who up to now had pretended to be amused at the girl's story in order to hide the fact that he was troubled by it, showed his anxiety by marching immediately into the outer room and meeting the stranger face to face. One look at him was quite enough to prove the wild guess of a man in love. This very well-dressed little man with a pointed black beard, clever eyes, and neat fingers, could be none other than the man just described to him: Isidore Smythe, who had made a fortune out of servants made of metal. Each man looked at the other, and immediately each understood the other's feelings for the girl.

Mr Smythe, however, made no mention of their rivalry, but said simply and loudly: "Has Miss Hope seen that thing on the window?"

"On the window?" repeated Angus in surprise.

"There's no time to explain the other things," said the rich man shortly. "There's a matter here that we have to look into."

He pointed his polished walking stick at the window. Angus

was astonished to see that a long piece of paper had been stuck along the front of the glass. This had certainly not been on the window when he had looked through it some time before. He followed Smythe outside into the street, and found that a narrow piece of paper about a yard and a half long had been carefully stuck along the glass outside, and on this had been written in irregular letters: "If you marry Smythe, he will die."

"Laura," said Angus, as he put his big red head into the shop, "you're not mad."

"It's the writing of that fellow Welkin," said Smythe. "I haven't seen him for years, but he's always worrying me. Five times in the last two weeks he's had threatening letters left at my flat, and I can't even find out who leaves them, and certainly not whether it's Welkin himself. The doorkeeper of the flats swears that no suspicious characters have been seen; and here he has stuck this paper on a shop window, while the people in the shop——"

"Quite so," said Angus modestly, "while the people in the shop were having tea. Well, sir, let me tell you I am pleased with your common sense in dealing so directly with the matter. We can talk about other things afterwards. The fellow cannot be very far off yet, for I swear there was no paper there when I went last to the window, ten or fifteen minutes ago. But he's too far off to be followed, as we don't even know the direction. If you'll take my advice, Mr Smythe, you'll put this at once in the hands of some detective, private rather than public. I know an extremely clever fellow, who has set up business in a place five minutes from here in your car. His name's Flambeau, and although his youth was a bit wild, he's a strictly honest man now, and his brains are worth money. He lives in Lucknow Flats, Hampstead."

"That's strange," said the little man, and raised his eyebrows. "I live myself in Himalaya Flats which are round the corner. Perhaps you might care to come with me. I can go to my rooms and sort out these strange Welkin letters, while you run round and get your friend the detective."

"You're very good," said Angus politely. "Well, the sooner we act the better."

Both men said goodbye to the girl and jumped into the fast little car. As Smythe drove and they turned the corner of the street, Angus was amused to see an immense advertisement of "Smythe's Silent Service" with a picture of a machine like a human being, except that it had no head. The machine carried a cooking-pan and underneath it were the words, "A Cook who is Never Bad-tempered".

"I use them in my own flat," said the little, black-bearded man with a laugh, "partly for advertisement, and partly for real convenience. Honestly, these big clockwork toys of mine do bring you coals or wine quicker than any live servants I've ever known, if you know which button to press. But I will also admit that such servants have their disadvantages, too."

"Indeed?" said Angus. "Is there something that they can't do?"

"Yes," replied Smythe. "They can't tell me who left those threatening letters at my flat."

The man's motorcar was small and quick like himself; in fact like his silent servants it was his own invention. Soon they turned a corner and were in the street which contained Himalaya Flats. Opposite the flats was a bushy garden, and some way below that ran a canal. As the car swept into the street it passed on one corner a man selling hot, roasted nuts. At the other end of the street, Angus could just see the blue figure of a policeman walking slowly. These were the only human shapes in that quiet scene.

The little car arrived at the right house with great speed, and Smythe got out very quickly. He immediately asked the door-keeper and another servant who was wearing no coat, whether anybody or anything had passed these officials since he had last made inquiries. Then he and the slightly confused Angus climbed the stairs, till they reached the top floor.

"Just come in for a minute," said Smythe. "I want to show you those Welkin letters. Then perhaps you will run round the corner and bring your friend." He pressed a button hidden in the wall, and the door opened by itself.

It opened on a long, wide outer room, of which the only unusual appearance was the rows of half-human machines that stood up on both sides. They were like the figures which tailors use. Like these figures, they had no heads, and like them, too, their chests and shoulders seemed to be slightly too large. But otherwise they were not much more like a human figure than any machine at a railway station that is about human height. They had two great hooks like arms for carrying trays, and they were painted bright green, or red, or black, so that the owner could recognise them. In every other way they were only machines and nobody would have looked twice at them. On this occasion, at least, nobody did. For between the two rows of these machines lay something more interesting than most of the machines in the world. It was a white piece of paper written on in red ink. The quick little inventor seized it up almost as soon as the door flew open. He handed it to Angus without a word. The red ink on it was actually not dry, and the message was: "If you have been to see her today, I shall kill you."

There was a short silence, and then Isidore Smythe said quietly: "Would you like a drink? I rather feel as if I should."

"No thank you. I should like to see Flambeau," said Angus miserably.

"Good," said the other quite cheerfully. "Bring him round here as quickly as you can."

But as Angus closed the front door behind him, he saw Smythe push back a button, and one of the clockwork figures moved smoothly from its place and slid along the floor carrying a tray with drinks on it. There did seem something a little extraordinary about leaving the little man alone among those dead servants, who were coming to life as the door closed.

Six steps down from Smythe's flat, the servant with no coat was doing something with a bucket. Angus stopped and made him promise, by giving him money, to stay there until his return with the detective, and to watch carefully any kind of stranger who came up those stairs. He hurried downstairs to the front hall and got the same promise from the doorkeeper. Angus learned from him that there was no back door. Not content with this, he caught the policeman and persuaded him to stand opposite the entrance and watch it. Then, last of all, he paused an instant to buy some hot, roasted nuts. He inquired how long the nutseller intended to stay in the neighbourhood.

The nutseller turned up the collar of his coat and told him that he would probably be moving soon, as he thought that it was going to snow. Indeed, the evening was growing grey and cold, but Angus managed to persuade him to remain where he was.

"Keep yourself warm with your own nuts," he said eagerly. "Eat up your whole stock; I'll pay you well for them. I'll give you a pound if you'll wait here till I come back, and then tell me whether any man, woman, or child has gone into that house where the doorkeeper is standing."

He then walked away, with a last look at the house. "I've made a ring round that room, anyhow," he said. "All four of them can't be friends of Welkin."

Lucknow Flats was lower down the same hill on which Himalaya Flats stood. Mr Flambeau's flat was on the ground floor. Flambeau, who was a friend of Angus's, received him in a little private room behind his office. It was ornamented with swords and weapons of all kinds, strange objects from the East, bottles of Italian wine, ancient cooking pots and a grey cat. With him in the room was a small, dusty-looking priest who did not look quite right in these surroundings.

"This is my friend, Father Brown," said Flambeau. "I've often wanted you to meet him. Splendid weather, this; a little cold for people from the south like me."

"Yes, I think it will keep clear," said Angus as he sat down.

"No," said the priest quietly; "it has begun to snow."

And indeed, as he spoke, the first snow began to fall gently across the darkening window.

"Well," said Angus, seriously, "I'm afraid I've come on business, and rather frightening business, too. The fact is, Flambeau, very close to your house here is a fellow who badly needs your help. He is frequently being threatened by an invisible enemy — a man whom nobody has ever seen." Angus went on to tell the whole story of Smythe and Welkin. He began with Laura's story, and went on with his own; the odd laugh at the corner of two empty streets; the strange clear words spoken in an empty room. Flambeau grew more and more interested, and the little priest seemed to be forgotten like a piece of furniture. When the story came to the piece of paper stuck on the window, Flambeau rose and seemed to fill the room with his immense shoulders.

"If you don't mind," he said, "I think that you'd better tell me the rest on the shortest road to this man's house. It seems to me, somehow, that we must not waste any time."

"Delighted," said Angus and he also got up. "Though he is safe enough for the present, for I've set four men to watch the only door to his house."

They went out into the street, with the small priest following after them like a little, faithful dog. He merely said, in a cheerful way, like one making conversation, "How quickly the snow gets thick on the ground."

As they walked along the streets which were already white with snow, Angus finished his story. By the time they reached the street where Smythe lived, he had time to turn his attention to the four guards whom he had left there. The nutseller, both before and after he had received a pound, swore that he had watched the door and seen no visitor enter. The policeman was even more sure. He said that he had had experience of criminals of all kinds, both well-dressed and in rags. He wasn't so foolish as to expect suspicious characters to look suspicious. He had looked out for anybody, and there had been nobody. And when all three men gathered round the doorkeeper, who stood there smiling, the answer was even more certain.

"I've got a right to ask any man, rich or poor, what he wants in these flats," said the doorkeeper, "and I'll swear there's been nobody to ask since this gentleman went away."

The unimportant Father Brown, who stood back and looked modestly at the ground, said quietly: "Has nobody been up and down stairs, then, since the snow began to fall? It began while we were all round at Flambeau's."

"Nobody has been here, sir. You can believe me," said the official.

"Then I wonder what that is?" said the priest and looked hard at the ground.

The others all looked down also. Flambeau laughed loudly in surprise. For there was no doubt that down the middle of the entrance guarded by the doorkeeper, actually between his stretched legs, there ran a pattern of footprints in the white snow.

"Good heavens!" cried Angus; "the Invisible Man!"

Without another word he turned and ran up the stairs with Flambeau following him; but Father Brown still stood and looked about him in the snow-covered street, as if he had lost interest in his inquiry.

Flambeau clearly wanted to break the door down with his big shoulder; but Angus, with more reason, if less imagination, felt about on the frame of the door till he found the invisible button. The door swung slowly open.

The hall had grown darker, although it was still lit here and there by the red light of the setting sun. One or two of the machines had been moved from their places for this or that purpose, and stood here and there about the half-dark room. But in the middle of them all, exactly where the paper with the red ink had lain, there lay something that looked very like red ink spilled out of a bottle. But it was not red ink.

Flambeau simply said, "Murder." He ran into the flat and explored every corner and cupboard of it in five minutes. But if he expected to find a dead body, he found none. Isidore Smythe simply was not in the place, either dead or alive. After a careful search, the two men met each other in the outer hall. "My friend," said Flambeau, speaking French in his excitement, "not only is the murderer invisible, but he also makes the murdered man invisible."

Angus looked round the dark room full of the figures of the machines and trembled. One of them stood over the bloodstain. Perhaps he had been called by the dead man an instant before he fell. One of the hooks that it used for arms was a little lifted, and Angus had the terrible fancy that Smythe's own iron child had struck him down. The machines had attacked their master. But even if this were true, what had they done with him?

"Eaten him," his imagination suggested. He felt sick for a moment at the idea of the broken human remains swallowed and crushed into those clockwork figures without heads.

With an effort he became calm, and said to Flambeau, "The poor fellow has just disappeared completely. That kind of happening does not belong to this world."

"There is only one thing to be done." said Flambeau. "Whether it belongs to this world or the other, I must go down and talk to my friend."

He went down the stairs and passed the man with the bucket, who once again said that he had let no stranger pass. The doorkeeper and the nutseller also swore again that they had been watchful. But when Angus looked round for his fourth guard, he could not see him, and called out: "Where's the policeman?"

"I beg your pardon," said Father Brown. "That is my fault. I have just sent him down the road for something."

"Well, we want him back soon," said Angus, "for the poor man upstairs has not only been murdered, but wiped out."

"How?" asked the priest.

"Father," said Flambeau after a pause, "I believe it's more easily understood by a priest than a detective. No friend or enemy has entered the house, but Smythe is gone, as if stolen by spirits. If that has a natural explanation, I——"

As he spoke he was interrupted by an unusual sight. The big, blue policeman came round the corner of the street running. He came straight up to Father Brown.

"You're quite right, sir," he said, out of breath, "they've just found poor Mr Smythe's body in the canal down below."

Angus put his hand wildly to his head. "Did he run down and drown himself?" he asked.

"He never came down, I'll swear," said the policeman, "and he wasn't drowned either, for he died of a great wound over the heart."

"And yet you saw no one enter?" said Flambeau.

"Let us walk down the road a little," said the priest.

As they reached the other end of the street, he said suddenly: "Stupid of me! I forgot to ask the policeman something. I wonder if they found a light brown bag."

"Why a light brown bag?" asked Angus, astonished.

"Because if it is a bag of any other colour, the case must begin again," said Father Brown. "But if it was a light brown bag, why, the case is finished."

"I am pleased to hear it," said Angus. "It hasn't begun, so far as I am concerned."

They were walking quickly down the long road. Father Brown was leading in silence. At last he said, "Well, I'm afraid you'll think it so dull and ordinary. Have you ever noticed this — that people never answer what you say? They answer what you mean — or what they think you mean. Suppose one lady says to another in a country house, 'Is anybody staying with you?' the lady doesn't answer, 'Yes; five servants' even though one of the servants may be in the room. She says: 'There is *nobody* staying with us.' She means nobody of the sort you mean. But suppose a doctor who is inquiring into a disease which is spreading in the neighbourhood asks, 'Who is staying in the house?' Then the lady will remember the five servants. All language is used like that. You never get a question answered exactly, even when you get it answered truly. When these four quite honest men said that nobody had gone into the building, they did not really mean that *no man* had gone into the building. They meant no man whom they could suspect of being the criminal. A man did go into the building, and did come out of it, but they never noticed him."

"An invisible man?" inquired Angus with raised eyebrows.

"A man who was invisible to the mind," said Father Brown.

A minute or two after he went on in a modest voice, like a man who is thinking out what he has to say. "Of course, you can't think of such a man, until you do think of him. That's the way in which he is so clever. But I came to think of him through two or three little things in the story that Mr Angus told us. First, there was the fact that Mr Welkin went for long walks. And then there were the two things the young lady said — things that couldn't be true. Don't get annoyed," he added hastily when he noticed a sudden movement of Angus's head. "She thought that they were true all right, but they couldn't be true. A person *can't* be quite alone in a street a second before she receives a letter. She can't be quite alone in a street when she starts to read a letter which she has just received. There must be somebody quite near her. He must be invisible to the mind."

"Why must there be somebody near her?" asked Angus.

"Because," said Father Brown, "somebody must have brought her the letter."

"Do you really mean to say," asked Flambeau eagerly, "that Welkin carried his rival's letter to his lady?"

"Yes," said the priest. "Welkin carried his rival's letters to his lady. You see, he had to."

"Oh, this will drive me mad," cried Flambeau. "Who is this fellow? What does he look like? What is the usual dress of a man who is invisible to the mind?"

"He is dressed in red, blue and gold," replied the priest immediately, "and in these striking, and even showy clothes, he entered Himalaya Flats in front of eight human eyes. He killed Smythe, and came down into the street again carrying the dead body in his arms——"

"Sir," cried Angus, "are you mad, or am I?"

"You are not mad," said Father Brown, "only you do not always observe things very closely. You have not noticed such a man as this, for example."

He took three quick steps forward, and put his hand on the shoulder of an ordinary postman who was hurrying past them unnoticed under the shade of the trees.

"Nobody notices postmen, somehow," he said thoughtfully. "Yet they have feelings like other men. They even carry bags where a small body can be hidden quite easily."

The postman, instead of turning naturally, had jumped with surprise and fallen against the garden fence. He was a thin fair-bearded man of very ordinary appearance, but as he turned a frightened face over his shoulder, he looked at all three men with a terrible squint.

Flambeau went back to his flat, since he had many things to attend to. John Turnbull Angus went back to the young lady at the shop, with whom he manages to be very comfortable. But Father Brown walked those snow-covered hills under the stars for many hours with a murderer. What they said to each other will never be known.

The Case of the Thing that Whimpered
by Dennis Wheatley

It would have been hard to find two men more different in appearance or way of living than the pair who were crossing the sunny garden of old Mark Hemmingway's home at Oyster Bay, Long Island.

Bruce was the old man's nephew. He was six feet two inches tall, with thick black hair and a strong good-looking face. He was a clever international lawyer. His companion, Neils Orsen, a delicate little man with large blue eyes, like those of a Siamese cat, was a Swede. He had chosen to spend his life in the study of ghosts and spirits.

When their ship, the SS *Orion*, was three days out from England they had discovered that they had worked very close to one another in London. It was Orsen's first trip to the United States, and Bruce had invited him to spend at least a week at Oyster Bay to see what a real American home was like. They had come straight out to Long Island after the ship had arrived that morning.

Bruce pointed to a heavy, grey-haired figure lying in a chair outside the house. "There's Uncle Mark, taking his usual Sunday afternoon rest."

"Then please let us not wake him," Orsen said.

"No, we won't do that; tea will be out in a minute, and he'll wake up then."

They lowered themselves quietly into basket-chairs, and while Orsen leant back and closed his eyes, content to enjoy the sweet-scented air of the garden, the big American bent down to pick up a newspaper from the grass. He loved facts and could never resist the opportunity to get information.

His eyes wandered over the page. There was more trouble in Europe, but that was nothing new. The daughter of the steel industry owner, Morgenfeld, had been kidnapped, and the reward which was being offered for the return of six-year-old Angela had been increased to half a million dollars. She had been missing now for nearly two months. From her photographs she seemed to be a very pretty child.

Suddenly Uncle Mark began to make strange noises in his sleep.

"Wake him," said Orsen. "Wake him at once."

Bruce leant over and shook him slightly. "Wake up, Uncle, Wake up!"

Mark Hemmingway gave a little cry, sat up and looked at them.

"Hello! So you've arrived. It's good to see you again, Bruce. And this is Mr Orsen whom you telegraphed me about, eh?"

Orsen smiled, "I am sorry if we woke you, sir, but you were having a bad dream, were you not?"

"Bad dream! Why, yes. How did you know?"

"That was not difficult — the noise that you were making. But I know quite a lot about dreams and I'll try to explain yours if you care to tell me what it was about."

"It's that storehouse. I can't get the place out of my thoughts." His nephew looked puzzled.

"Yes, yes, storehouse. But never mind my troubles. I don't want to tire Mr Orsen the moment that he has arrived, and it was only the usual confused bad dream, anyhow."

"His real interests are ghost-hunting," Bruce smiled, "and though I don't think we'll find any ghosts round here, I hope that we'll be able to give him a good time."

"We'll certainly do our best," replied Mr Hemmingway. "But as for ghosts, I just don't believe in such things, although I've had cause enough to believe in anything these last few weeks."

"Thanks, Mr Hemmingway," answered Orsen. "It is most kind of you to receive me in your beautiful home. But what you say naturally excites my curiosity. I'm not surprised that you don't believe in ghosts because they really appear very rarely. The things which people believe to be ghosts are nearly always the working of the imagination or tricks which have been produced for a special purpose. Do tell me what it is that has recently caused you so much worry."

"It's the terrible events, that have happened one after the other in this storehouse that I was dreaming about just now."

Bruce sat back and said, "Let us have the details."

His uncle hesitated for a moment, and then with a look at the stranger, he began: "As Bruce may have told you, I'm the director of one of the biggest chains of shops in New York. In recent months we have had to take a new storehouse in East 20th Street. It's not a good place because it's a long way from my shops and is built among blocks of poor flats down in the lower East Side. But we needed it quickly and it was the best our agents could find. The building stands ten floors high, and the night-watchman has two rooms on the top floor. They are an office and a sitting room. These are connected by a short gallery, one side of which is formed by the outer wall and the other is open except for a single handrail so that the guard can look down upon the whole storehouse. The two rooms and the gallery are built on a kind of raised stage which can only be reached from the ground by some iron stairs. I'm giving you these details because the happenings in this place have provided a puzzle which the cleverest detectives in New York have failed to solve. But stop me if you're not interested."

"No, no; please go on."

"Right, then. The morning after we took the place the night-watchman was found on the ground floor badly hurt, and half-dead. There had been no robbery; all the doors and windows were still locked. Yet somehow this unfortunate man had been attacked, while he was checking the storehouse, in the most violent manner by someone or something that has the most unbelievable strength."

"Something! Really, Uncle Mark! We don't have ghosts in New York," Bruce interrupted with a half-smile twisting his mouth. "What did the man say when he gained consciousness?"

"The poor fellow could tell us very little. The last thing he remembered was just having left the sitting room to make his midnight check. He said that he paused a moment outside because he thought he heard a strange whimpering sound like that of an animal in pain, when suddenly the whole place seemed to melt — that's how he described it — and he found himself falling through the air to fall on the stone floor below. He knew nothing until he woke up in hospital."

"Surely he can give some description of the thing that attacked him?" Bruce said.

"No. In the poor light he saw nothing. He had no time to look round. He says that his legs bent under him and he was thrown with great force forward and down."

"That doesn't make sense."

"It's the best description that he could give us and we were lucky to get that, as his terrible experience has had a bad effect on his brain." Mark Hemmingway paused as two servants came out with tea trays. When they had gone and he had poured out some tea for his guests, he went on: "But that isn't all. We put a second night-watchman in, and on the third night of his stay he was found just like the other, only his neck was broken besides other terrible wounds; so he had no story to tell."

"And the police, what did they say?" Orsen asked.

"They discovered nothing in their search, absolutely nothing. There was not a single sign of any living thing ever having entered the building after it had been closed for the night. They did suggest one thing, however. It was this: that as this place had been empty for three years before we took it, a group of criminals might have been using it for unlawful purposes; and by these attacks on night-watchmen they hoped to frighten the new owners away. That was the suggestion, but the police could not produce any proof that the storehouse had ever been used for anything, and, although hundreds of people who live in that crowded neighbourhood were questioned, not one of them could remember ever having seen a car of any kind, which might contain stolen goods, drive up to the place by day or night, until we arrived."

"Why should they?" Bruce asked. "People who live down on the lower East Side don't generally regard the police as their friends. If criminals are working there, no one is going to risk being shot by them."

"That's so. I think you're right about that. Anyhow, after the death of the second watchman, it was very difficult to find another. However, two days ago we employed a really strong man who knew nothing of the history of the place. This morning he was found living, but terribly hurt. His face was beaten in, one arm was twisted behind his back and broken, and his chest was crushed. It was just as though some great force had picked him up and thrown him against the storehouse floor like a toy. In hospital, when he was conscious, he could scarcely talk. All he could tell the police captain was: 'Something whimpered at me — something whimpered, and then — and then I was thrown through the air.'"

"So they both heard the strange whimpering," Orsen said thoughtfully. "What did the police chief have to say about that?"

"Nothing. He couldn't explain it at all. They are not even sure yet of the exact place where the attacks were made. The first man doesn't *remember* going down to the main storehouse by the iron stairs; but that doesn't mean much, as there were no signs of a struggle in the gallery, and all three bodies were found below. One of the youngest of the policemen who are working on these crimes did suggest, although he felt a little foolish about it, that there might be ghosts in the place and that this is the work of some sort of devil. Quite honestly, I have an odd feeling that the man might be right. No human has the strength to beat men as violently as that. Even if he had, they would remember something of what had happened to them."

"I see," said Neils Orsen. "Of course there are rare cases when evil spirits take on violent and dangerous strength. But I'm more ready to believe the first suggestion, that your storehouse has been used for unlawful purposes, and that somebody is particularly anxious to frighten you into giving it up. . . . Still, I should very much like to try to solve the mystery. May I take on the duties of night-watchman tonight?"

"Good heavens, no! You're my guest. I cannot allow — well, anyone like yourself to spend a night in that place alone."

Orsen smiled. "I see you're thinking of my size, Mr Hemmingway. But I should carry a gun. We could also have a police guard outside the building, and if they are criminals who are doing this, my shots would bring immediate help. However, if it really is a ghost or an evil spirit, I am far better able to deal with it than the toughest policeman in New York."

"No, no. You've never met the sort of criminals we have in this country. They are killers and they would murder you before the police even got through the door. I'll tell you what I will do, though. I'll take you and Bruce to have a look round the place tomorrow afternoon."

The three of them, with a police officer, made a careful search of the storehouse, but they found nothing fresh. The policeman was sure that the attacks had been made on the floor of the storehouse, but Orsen thought that they had happened while the watchman was up in the gallery, because the only man who could give even a partly sensible account of what had happened could not remember coming down the iron stairs.

For this reason it was up in the gallery that he put the scientific instruments that he had brought with him. These were two cameras with flashlights, and wires which would work them if anyone crossed the gallery, and a sound recording-machine of his own invention, which was so sensitive, he said, that it could pick up voices from the world of spirits.

The police officer watched his preparation with open scorn, while Hemmingway and Bruce only hid their disbelief out of politeness. But Orsen declared, with great confidence, that he meant to find out whether the attacker was a ghost or a man.

On the following morning they visited the storehouse again. The locks on the doors and windows had not been touched — yet Orsen's two cameras and his recording-machine were no longer up in the gallery. They lay broken to pieces on the floor below.

The little Swede began to collect the bits and with Bruce's

help put them all in a bag. But although the cameras could not help them, they found, when they returned to Oyster Bay, that the material on the recording-machine was unbroken. Orsen tested it on another machine.

For a moment a low, whimpering cry shook in the pleasantly sunny room, and seemed to fill it with the presence of something evil. Then the sound suddenly stopped.

"Well, the watchman certainly didn't imagine that!" said Bruce with a rather frightened laugh.

"No," Orsen's pale blue eyes filled with a sudden light; "and that's not the sort of noise a killer makes when he is about to murder someone. I really believe now that we're on the track of an *Ab-human*."

"What is that?" asked Bruce.

"It's not a ghost in the ordinary sense at all. By that I mean it's not the spirit of a dead man that is bound to the earth, but a bodiless force — something that has somehow made its way up out of the Great Depths and found a gateway by which it can get back into this world. Such appearances are very rare, but to a scientist like myself extremely interesting. Now nothing can prevent me from going back to the storehouse this evening and passing the night there."

"I won't allow you to do that alone," Bruce said quickly.

"I shall be delighted to have your company," Orsen smiled.

Orsen made careful preparations for the night's watch, because he knew that Bruce might have to face great danger. Both carried guns in case the ghost was found to be human after all. Both also had charms of proved power against evil spirits. Bruce felt like laughing at such protections, but the little man was so serious about them that Bruce hid his amusement.

At nine o'clock they went to the storehouse. The place was badly lit and every packing-case seemed to throw the shadow of some terrible being after them as they walked.

"Brrr — I don't envy any man who has to stay here all night, whether there are ghosts or not," said Bruce.

"It'll be more cheerful upstairs in the watchman's sitting

room," Orsen said quietly. When they had climbed the iron stairs he began to explain his plans to Bruce.

"I mean to go round the whole place every hour, but I want you to remain in this room, Bruce. You are not to leave it whatever happens. You will stay by the door and watch the gallery outside with your gun ready and protect my back each time I go downstairs. If you see only a shadow, shoot instantly. Light will always drive back the Powers of Darkness, at least for a moment. The flash from your gun will give me just enough time to say the words which will protect us against evil spirits."

At ten o'clock Orsen went round the storehouse for the first time. Bruce stood in the doorway of the sitting room and guarded the gallery with his gun, until his little friend was hidden from sight in the shadows. He then returned to his seat in the room. A quarter of an hour later, Orsen quietly appeared again. Bruce jumped quickly to his feet and asked. "Well?"

"No, nothing," replied Orsen.

Conversation was difficult. The frightening silence all round them seemed even to forbid a whisper. The sun had shone on the roof all day and the heat of the room was uncomfortable. Both men were sitting without coats on.

The minutes dragged on. Eleven o'clock came at last, and once again the little Swede went out into the unfriendly shadows beyond the warm sitting room, while Bruce watched from the door. Once again he returned with nothing to report.

Time seemed to stand still. Bruce suddenly began to think of the people in the town only a few miles away who were laughing and talking without a worry in the world. They would sleep in warm, comfortable beds, while he sat waiting for some terrible, unknown thing to come out of the half-darkness, violently attack him and afterwards throw him away like a broken toy.

He shook himself. He was certainly not a coward, and if his gun and strength could have been of any use, there would have been no fear in his heart. But the calm little man opposite him sincerely believed in ghosts and spirits, and had even told him of their terrible power against human beings.

The minutes crept on. Suddenly Orsen moved uncomfortably in his seat. His long, thin fingers tapped on his knees, and Bruce watched him with quick anxiety. Then a low whimpering cry broke the stillness of the quiet room.

Instantly Orsen jumped to his feet and ran to the door. As he ran he called aloud some Latin words from an ancient prayer for protection against evil spirits. Bruce took hold of his gun and followed. As Orsen stepped out on to the gallery the whole thing seemed to start to fall at a sharp angle beneath him. He almost lost his balance. His legs were unable to support him, and he was violently thrown forward into space.

At the same instant Bruce, who was still at the door of the sitting room, had seen that as the floor fell sideways so the wall behind moved downward at right angles to it. Another moment and the block of wall falling outward would fill the place where the gallery floor had been. In the dark space behind the falling wall Bruce saw a shadowy shape. His gun fired with a bright red flame until it was empty. There was a cry of pain and the wall began to fall back again and brought the floor of the gallery up with it.

"Neils! Neils!" Bruce cried as he looked out into the half darkness. To his great relief a cry came back to him. By the grace of God, Orsen had managed to hold on to the single rail of the gallery as he was thrown outwards. It was a frightening moment as he hung there by one hand, eighty feet above the stone floor below. But as the wall fell back into place, the floor of the gallery moved with it and brought him back to safety. Bruce, whose face was grey and covered in sweat, pulled him into the sitting room, and for a few moments they both stood there breathing heavily.

When their strength returned, they set to work to solve the mystery of the hidden entrance. With the help of an iron bar they managed to make the block of wall start moving down, and they saw the floor of the gallery immediately start to fall as they did so.

"That's what happened to the unfortunate night-watchmen!"

Orsen said, "An eighty-foot drop! No wonder they remembered nothing and were beaten to pieces."

"Come on! Let's see what's in here," Bruce whispered and pointed to the dark space which the opening of the wall had left. As he stepped forward, his foot touched something. He turned the beam of his flash-lamp in that direction and bent down. He saw that it was the body of a man. Together they dragged it into the light. It was not a pretty sight. The man had clearly not been very fond of soap and water. He was bleeding badly from several gun-shot wounds and was quite dead.

"I suppose I must have killed him." said Bruce slowly. "I wonder what he was doing."

"I wonder. Clearly he has been coming and going to this secret room for some time and entering it by a hidden door. Then when your uncle's people moved in he thought he would frighten them by killing your night-watchmen. He just had to wait for the poor fellows to begin their midnight check and then pull a handle. Too simple!"

Suddenly the whimpering came again. Bruce felt the hair on the back of his neck stand up, but Orsen calmly turned on his torch and flashed it round the room. Its beam fell upon a child sitting frightened against some old bags.

"Angela Morgenfeld!" cried Bruce in surprise. With two steps he reached her, and picked up the thin, frightened little thing in his arms. "Orsen," he cried, "do you realise that this is the steel-owner's daughter, who was kidnapped over two months ago?"

He laughed then with mixed relief and excitement. "That man whom I killed must have been coming in every night over the roof to feed her. And this poor child is your great *Ab-human*."

Orsen smiled. "I would rather have found her, though, than the most interesting spirit from another world. But wait until we are back in England next month and I'll certainly show you a real ghost."

Bruce laughed. "I'll be with you."

Questions

Questions on factual details

The Blue Cross
1 What was the one thing which Flambeau could not hide?
2 Why did Valentin put his cup of coffee down very quickly?
3 Who rolled the shopkeeper's apples all over the street?
4 What did the priest leave in the sweet shop?
5 What was inside the brown-paper parcel which Flambeau opened?
6 What were the two things Father Brown did to test Flambeau's intentions?

Philomel Cottage
1 How old was Alix when her cousin died and left her a few thousand pounds?
2 Why was Alix surprised to see the gardener?
3 What was the first secret that Alix ever kept from her husband?
4 What fact about Gerald convinced Alix that he was Charles Lemaitre?
5 What was Gerald carrying when Alix saw him returning to the house?
6 Why did Gerald complain about the taste of the coffee which Alix gave him?
7 Where did Alix tell Gerald she had worked during the war?
8 Who was with Dick Windyford when he came to Philomel Cottage?

The Heel
1 When did the servant find out that his master was dead?

2 Where was the American staff officer when he wrote a note to Mr Harris?

3 How long did Sergeant Place have to wait for the American staff officer?

4 Why did Sergeant Place want Spencer to see the man in the kitchen?

The Unlucky Theatre
1 What was the name of the owner of the theatre?
2 What did Fernaghan see while he was drinking his coffee?
3 What did Mrs Lang do after her husband was killed?

The Great Idea of Mr Budd
1 What colour was the hair of the man who came into Mr Budd's shop?
2 What did the stranger do as soon as he had read the article in *The Evening Messenger*?
3 Where did Mr Budd go after he caught a number 24 bus?
4 Why didn't the passenger in cabin number 36 want to come out of his cabin?
5 What was the name of the first person to come into Mr Budd's shop after *The Evening Messenger* printed the story of his Great Idea?

The Mezzotint
1 When was the parcel delivered to Mr Williams's office?
2 Where did Mr Williams put the picture before he went to bed?
3 What had changed in the picture when Nisbet looked at it?
4 What was Mr Williams's servant doing when Mr Williams and his friends returned to his rooms?
5 Where is the picture kept now?

Family Affair
1 What year did the *Mary Celeste* mystery take place?

2   What time did Bertram Heskith visit the McGills on the morning they disappeared?
3   Who lived in 33 Chestnut Grove?
4   What was the only thing that seemed to interest Mr Campion in 29 Chestnut Grove?
5   What was in the hut at the bottom of the garden?
6   How much money had the McGills won?

The Invisible Man
1   What was the name of the inn which Laura's father owned?
2   What was the real reason Laura refused to marry both Isidore Smythe and James Welkin?
3   What was the advice which Angus gave to Mr Smythe?
4   Who were the four people Angus asked to watch out for strangers at Mr Smythe's flat?
5   Who was with Flambeau in his room?
6   Where was Mr Smythe's body found?
7   What were the colours of the clothes that Mr Welkin wore?

The Case of the Thing that Whimpered
1   Where was Mark Hemmingway's home?
2   How many floors did the new storehouse have?
3   How many night-watchmen had worked at the storehouse?
4   What did Orsen put in the gallery on his first visit to the storehouse?
5   How often did Orsen plan to go round the storehouse during the night?
6   Who was whimpering in the storehouse?

Questions on the stories as a whole

1   "A simple priest." Do you agree with Father Brown's description of himself in "The Blue Cross"?
2   Pretend you are Flambeau, and describe your conversation with Father Brown on the seat in Hampstead Heath.

3   "The man's a complete stranger to you. You know nothing about him." Describe what Alix discovers about her husband.

4   How do Alix's feelings towards her husband change during the story "Philomel Cottage"?

5   Why do you think Gerald believed that Alix had poisoned him?

6   Imagine that you are Staff Officer Spencer and describe what happens when you visit Mr Harris's house.

7   "Mr Harris was quite a clever criminal." Is this true, in your opinion?

8   From the information in the story, what sort of person was Mr Budd?

9   What effect do the events of "The Great Idea of Mr Budd" have on Mr Budd's life?

10   Tell the story of "The Great Idea of Mr Budd" as if you were William Strickland.

11   Describe how the attitude of Mr Williams towards the picture changes during the story of "The Mezzotint".

12   "I should say now that it looks as if old Gawdy had managed the thing himself." What do you think?

13   Describe the character of Peter McGill.

14   What idea are we given of the character of Maureen McGill?

15   "I'm afraid you'll think it so dull and ordinary." What does Father Brown mean, and do you agree with his opinion of the case of "The Invisible Man"?

16   "You do not always observe things very closely." How is this shown to be true in the story of "The Invisible Man"?

17   What do we learn of the character of John Angus in the story "The Invisible Man"?

18   What does Mark Hemmingway feel about the events that have happened at his storehouse?

19   Why is Orsen certain that they are on the track of an *Abhuman*?

20   What does Orsen know about ghosts and spirits?

Glossary

agency a business that brings people in touch; **agent** = a person who represents a company

applaud to show approval by striking one's hands together

arrest to seize by the power of the law

barber a man who cuts men's hair and sometimes shaves them

basin a round container that is used for holding food or liquids

butcher a person who works in a shop which sells meat

cabin a room in a ship, usually used for sleeping

canal an artificial waterway dug in the ground

cellar an underground room

curious eager to know or learn, especially about something mysterious; **curiosity** = the desire to know

dye to change the colour of something with a chemical substance

football pools a competition in which large amounts of money can be won

gallery an upper floor built out from an inner wall, open on one side

greed a strong desire to have a lot of something; **greedy** = full of greed

hairdresser a person whose job is to cut people's hair

heath an open piece of wild land where grass and other plants grow

heel an unpleasant or dishonourable man

inch a unit for measuring length, equal to 2.54 cm

inn a small pub or hotel; **innkeeper** = a person who runs an inn

inspector a police officer of middle rank

invisible that cannot be seen

Irish Sweep (the) a horse race in which large amounts of money can be won by betting

kidnap to take someone away illegally

locksmith a person who makes or repairs locks

mezzotint the name given to a particular kind of print

nightingale a bird known for its beautiful song, sometimes called Philomel in poetry

puzzle a game in which parts must be fitted together correctly

puzzled uncertain how to explain or understand

razor a sharp instrument for removing hair

reputation an opinion held about someone or something by people in general

rival a person with whom one competes; **rivalry** = competition

scorn angry disrespect; **scornful** = showing that one feels scorn

Scotland Yard the main office of the London police

shilling a coin; in British currency before 1971, 20 shillings = £1

skeleton the structure consisting of all the bones in the human body

squint a disorder of the eyes causing them to look in two different directions

staff officer an officer who helps a high-ranking military commander

suspicion a belief that someone may be guilty or that something bad may exist; **suspicious** = causing one to suspect guilt

telegraph to send a message by sending radio signals

trunk call (old-fashioned British) a long-distance telephone call

waistcoat a garment without arms that is usually worn under a jacket

whimper to make small weak cries